TH

Russell Gary was a plague carrier, that feared and despised being, of which few were left east of the Mississippi river. He had been spared by some long chance of fate – or great cosmic error – when the entire United States east of the Mississippi was laid waste by bombs and a death-dealing virus. West of the river a terrified population was guarded vigilantly and ruthlessly from the contaminated East by the Army, who had blown all bridges, with a couple of heavily guarded exceptions.

It was this dilemma that faced Russell Gary; whether to contrive an escape back to civilisation, or to fight for a lone-wolf existence in the devastated land with the other wild survivors.

His final decision, and the action that ensues makes a superb novel of suspense and excitement.

Also by the same author, and available in Coronet Books:

Wild Talent
The Lincoln Hunters

The Long Loud Silence

Wilson Tucker

CORONET BOOKS
Hodder and Stoughton

First published in Great Britain 1953
by The Bodley Head Limited

Coronet edition 1980

British Library C.I.P.

Tucker. Wilson
The long loud silence.
I. Title
823' .9'IF PS3539. U324L/

ISBN 0-340-25087-9

The characters and situations in this book are entirely imaginary and bear no relation to any real person or actual happening

Printed and bound in Great Britain for Hodder and Stoughton Paperbacks, a division of Hodder and Stoughton Ltd., Mill Road, Dunton Green, Sevenoaks, Kent (Editorial Office: 47 Bedford Square, London, WC1 3DP) by Hunt Barnard Printing Ltd., Aylesbury, Bucks.

CHAPTER ONE

Gary hugged the shadows along the shore and waited for the sound of the shot, for the sharp crack of a carbine. The old woman had been a fool to think she could sneak across the bridge, either starved to the point of desperation or a fool. The darkness of the night couldn't hide her, not any more, not with the troops guarding the other end of the bridge with infra-red lamps and sniperscopes on their rifles.

This was the only bridge left intact along a six or seven hundred mile stretch of the Mississippi, and American troops would be concentrated in strength on the other end. The old woman had no more chance of slipping across to the Iowa shore than a snowball in a cyclotron.

Gary crawled around a concrete abutment and waited. He was careful not to show his body on the roadway, not to cross to the other side of the two-lane bridge. He was too far away from the troops to be in real danger, but some gun-happy soldier just might catch him in his 'scope and fire.

The old woman didn't know the army, didn't know their equipment as he did. In her foolish, hungry mind she must have thought she could cross over under cover of darkness. She should have known better; she should have known what to expect after a year of it. Or perhaps she no longer cared. The old woman surely knew she couldn't live to reach the other side. No one from the contaminated area crossed the Mississippi and lived more than a few seconds, a few minutes. If you were among the lucky millions living in the western two-thirds of the nation, you gave thanks to your god. But if you were among the unlucky thousands still struggling for an existence east of the river, you remained there until you died. There was no other choice, no other future.

Stay where you were and die slowly. Make an attempt to reach the clean, unbombed country west of the Mississippi and die quickly under the sights of a carbine. The trooper's heart might not be in it – he might hesitate the fraction of a second, but you'd die. No contamination cases wanted.

The rifle cracked in the blackness.

Gary lay still, waiting. There was no other sound for long minutes. He knew the routine, had watched it often in the daylight. Some soldier garbed in a white radiation suit would walk out on to the bridge, move the body with a toe of his boot, searching for a spark of life. If there was still movement he would put a pistol shot through her head. Finally he would pick up the body and hurl it over the guardrail.

He seemed to hear a faint splash. The wind was in the wrong direction and he couldn't be sure, but the hungry old woman was undoubtedly floating downstream by now.

He crawled off the bridge approach and sought the sanctuary of a near-by field, seeking out the hollow depression where he had been lying when the woman passed him half an hour before. Curiosity had made him follow her, the morbid curiosity of an onlooker who knows the game will end in disaster. She had been carrying no food, he saw that in his first swift scrutiny; had she been carrying anything to eat he would have forcibly taken it from her. But her arms had been bare and there were no bulges to her pockets. So he had let her go to the bridge, silently following for no real reason.

He had known what would happen to her, and surely she did. In all likelihood she no longer cared. You get so old, you grow so hungry – and finally you seek a way out. The bridge was always a way out. Or downstream where the bridges had been dynamited, a rowboat. The troops were continuously on the prowl and the river watch never ended.

Gary knew there were many thousands of them, a large portion of what remained of the United States Army, stationed all along the western bank of the Mississippi, all the way from the delta northward to Lake Winnibigoshish in Minnesota, and from that point still northward overland to Lake Winnipeg in Manitoba. Still north of that body of water, the Mounted Patrol or terrain stopped you.

He could have been among those lucky troops on the other side of the river, the safe side. If he hadn't got blind drunk a year ago. Hadn't wakened up in that hotel.

Corporal Russell Gary, with a Fifth Army patch on his shoulder and nothing more strenuous than recruitment duty in downstate Illinois. Veteran of the Salerno campaign – he lasted five days on the beach before shrapnel pushed him off; veteran of the French and German thrusts – he was promoted to a tech-sergeantcy in the early days of the Normandy invasion and busted again before he reached the Rhine. Experienced and unscrupulous black-marketeer, junior grade; turned a tidy sum dealing in military gasoline, rations, soap, foodstuffs. He elected to stay in the army after the war because he had no home to speak of, and on his thirtieth birthday he was celebrating ten years of khaki with a monumental binge.

He figured the army owed him a year's pay.

When he woke up he was on the wrong side of the river, the bombed and contaminated side . . .

CHAPTER TWO

Corporal Gary sneezed and opened his eyes.

The dirty wallpaper only half-clinging to the ceiling seemed ready to come loose and drop on him at any moment. He sneezed again and rolled his eyes to see the equally sad paper peeling from the side walls. The layer peeling off wore faded pink roses and below that was another of dirty blue feathers. A battered old telephone hung on the wall near the door, screwed to the cracking plaster. His rumpled trousers were on the floor beside the bed.

'Mother of Moses!' the corporal complained, 'another stinking firetrap.'

He fought away a nagging ache in his back and a dull pain in his head to sit up. The movement sent a fine cloud of dust flying, and he sneezed again. Instinctively he reached under the pillow for his wallet and dislodged a whisky bottle. Savagely throwing the pillow and the bottle across the room, he snatched up his trousers from the floor and searched the pockets. His wallet was tucked in one of them, empty.

The corporal shouted one word and hurled the wallet after the pillow and the bottle.

Swinging his legs to the floor, he swore loudly when his naked toes made contact rather violently with another bottle. Gary peered down at it, was vaguely disappointed to find it empty, and saw still another one lying part way under the bed.

'That,' he said to the dirty carpet, 'must have been one hell of a toot!'

The room contained a toilet and a wash basin in one corner, half concealed behind a wooden screen. Another empty floated in the stool. A thin layer of dust and powdered plaster lay over every surface. Gary twisted the single tap jutting out over the basin but no water came out. He repeated the single, shouted word with added emphasis and stalked across the room to the ancient wall telephone.

'Hey, down there! What the hell goes on here? I want some water.'

The instrument did not answer him.

'Hell of a note,' he complained, and let the earpiece bang against the wall. Behind the wallpaper some loose plaster dribbled down. 'Hell of a note.'

He stopped to survey the room. Except for the dust, it was no different from a dozen other cheap hotels he had previously frequented for one purpose or another. The room hadn't been cleaned for a week – and hell, he hadn't been sleeping that long. One or two days was the limit on this sort of thing. Say two days – and that was stretching it. He shoved a bottle with his toe and tried to recall events. Quite plainly he hadn't been miserly with the liquor – he must have pitched a king-sized bitch. Ten years in the damned army, thirty years old and still reasonably healthy, and if that didn't call for a birthday celebration, nothing did. So all right, he had shot the works. But he couldn't have been out for more than two days.

Somebody would have missed him by now, and he'd be on the carpet for sure.

'Hell of a note,' he said again and reached for his trousers.

They were the only article of clothing in the room. Gary searched carefully, quickly, his anger growing, but there were no shoes or socks, no underwear, shirt or cap. He pulled on the wrinkled trousers and kicked at the wallet, cursing the unknown thief who had robbed him and then stolen his clothing while he slept. In nothing but trousers he yanked open the bedroom door and strode into the narrow hall. His room number told him he was on the third floor.

Without hesitation he walked to the stairway, dust flying from the worn carpet with each angry footfall. Approaching the dimly lighted stairs, he passed a room whose door hung open and absently looked in.

Shocked, he stopped, took a step backward, and stared again. She lay naked on the bed.

Gary turned quickly, searched the hall behind him and the

stairway beneath, to find he was still alone. Silently then he moved just inside the room.

The room was dusty and unclean like his own, but it also held an offensive odour that stung his nostrils, an odour he had known and lived with long ago. The woman's clothing was scattered about the floor, her open and ransacked purse had been tossed under the bed. A cheap suitcase had been split open and thrown aside. Gary stared at her body.

She was a nondescript woman, thirty or forty years of age – it was difficult to tell now. Not pretty, not ugly, but obviously a tramp. She fitted into the cheap and smelly room, into the run-down hotel. There were old and new scars on her thin body, and a dried trickle of blood on one ear where an earring had been torn away.

Gary moved nearer the bed, ignoring the odour, to confirm his first startled suspicion. A G.I. bayonet protruded from between her bony ribs.

He hesitated only a second longer and ran from the room. The hallway remained empty. He sped for the stairs, half-jumping them in his eagerness to descend, to get away from the third floor. The second floor landing and corridor were equally bare of sound or movement and he continued down without pause, seeking the lobby.

It was a small lobby, dirty, dusty, empty.

'Hey,' he shouted nervously, 'wake up!' He ran to the desk. 'It's me, Corporal Gary!'

There was no answer, no appearance.

He hit the old desk with his fist, pounding on its scarred surface. Dust flew upward and he sneezed. The lobby remained empty of life. A calendar pad caught his eye and he snatched it up, blowing a fine film of dust from its surface. Wednesday, June 20th. The day after his birthday, the day after the evening on which he had begun the celebrated binge. But the calendar couldn't be right because he knew damned well he had not got drunk only the night before. That had been two or three days ago, maybe more, and he had slept it off upstairs. It *was* two or three days ago. The calendar had dust on it. To hell with the calendar!

He hurled the metal base and its papers through a lobby

window, hearing the shards of glass sprinkle the pavement outside.

'I'm in here!' he shouted after the calendar.

Silence.

In sudden anger he picked up a heavy inkwell from the desk and tossed it through a second window, with the same negative result. No one came to investigate. Gary waited until he had counted fifty, aloud, and turned away from the desk. Sunlight shining through the unwashed glass of a street door caught his eye. He crossed the lobby, pushed through the door and stood on the pavement outside. The hot sun felt good on his half naked body but the pavement was uncomfortable to his feet.

He saw only a mongrel dog trotting along the gutter. The dog and a car.

Gary ignored the dog and concentrated on the car. The nose and radiator of the car were rammed through a plate glass window of a clothing store, the front tyres flat and shredded where they had exploded upon violent contact with first the kerb and then the building. Both bumpers were crumpled and the windscreen cracked and shattered to the limit of its resistance. A window dummy had toppled forward across the hood, while within the car another lifeless body hung across the wheel, impaled. The odour he had found in the room upstairs was multiplied here on the street.

Gary walked slowly from the hotel, fighting to read some kind of sense into what he had found. The bomb crater stopped him, shocked him. And then he knew.

The round, uneven crater occupied the whole width of the street and a truck had tumbled into it, unable to stop. The driver of the truck was still in the cab, dead. Beyond that was another crater, and he quickly saw the signs of an air strike that had been so familiar eight to ten years before. Show windows shattered, buildings chipped and battered, the street a crazy tangle of cars and debris. The city had been bombed. Bombed while he slept like a drunken fool.

But bombs – here, in Illinois! Towns and cities like this were common in Italy, in France, in Germany. He had been through hundreds of them, fought through and helped raze scores of them – in Italy, in France, in Germany. But not here in Illinois! Who would bomb Illinois? Who would make war on the United States?

This was why the hotel was empty of life, this was why the murdered woman lay up there on the third floor bed. The city had been bombed, the survivors evacuated.

The survivors?

Gary ran along the street, searching for a living man. Some cars stood at the kerb, unoccupied, while others were smashed in their flight. None contained anything living. Debris littered the street and only an occasional breeze moved a bit of trash, a discarded newspaper. Eagerly he snatched up the newspaper, scanned the headlines. Nothing. The paper held no mention of war, no hint of war, no threat of a bombing, no clue or forewarning to any sort of catastrophe – to America. The front page and the others inside mirrored only the day-to-day violence of usual nature at home and abroad. The date?

Like the dusty calendar. Wednesday, June 20th. The day after his birthday.

He dropped the paper and ran to the nearest car, reached inside and snapped on the radio. The battery was dead. Running along the street, Gary paused at another car parked alongside the kerb, tried the radio. It hummed into life. The airwaves were dead – either dead or deliberately silent. He slowly worked the dial from one end to the other, hoping to catch even the faintest whisper of sound, a spoken word or a bit of music, but there was nothing.

He decided they were maintaining radio silence. The absence of living people around him was proof they had been evacuated, that authority still existed somewhere. But that authority was keeping a rigid silence on the air, still fearing attack. He turned off the radio and slumped in the seat, wondering what he should do.

He supposed he was technically classed as a deserter by this time – that or listed as missing in action. The absence of a comparatively unimportant recruiting corporal would be noticed after two or three days. But for the moment it didn't make much difference; sooner or later he would find a military post and report in. Where? Might as well go back to Chicago

– he was known there. How? He'd have to help himself to a car and drive – he rather doubted that trains would still be running. The enemy always goes for the rail lines first.

His feet burned. So first he'd have to find some shoes. And after that, something to eat . . .

Corporal Gary sat on the deserted kerb before a grocery store, watching the tired sun go down and eating his supper from an assortment of pilfered cans and jars. He had helped himself to the food, there being no one in the store to either help or hinder him. The absence of assistants led him to suspect the bombing had happened at night; the display windows were smashed and the door hung askew but there were no bodies within the store itself. The grocery offered itself to him.

The bread he passed by because it was beginning to glaze over with a green mould, the fruit and vegetables were inedible. The big refrigerators had been neutralised with the failure of electricity, and the meats, milk and cheeses within them made unsafe. Angrily he had slammed the doors on the odour. He had discovered and pulled from a slowly thawing freezer a whole chicken, which now lay wrapped in a bag on the pavement beside him. There had been other food in the freezing unit but they were much too hard to eat now, and did not represent the value of the chicken to his mind. They could wait. Cans, jars, and a wax-sealed box of crackers made up his meal. Unable to locate running water, he drank canned juices and bottled soda water.

And then he threw an empty can across the wide street, listening to its clatter in the stillness. When the noise had died away he ripped open a carton of cigarettes and lit one.

'A hell of a note!' he said to the oncoming evening.

A borrowed car stood at the kerb a few feet away, its radio humming. He had set the dial at what he thought to be one of the most popular Chicago wavebands, and let it run. As yet there had been no rewarding voice.

During the remainder of the afternoon he had driven around the town, ranging it from one end to the other in search of any living thing. He had found no one, the city was dead or deserted. It did occur to him belatedly that there might be someone there, someone who would hide at the sound of the approaching car. Looters, the thieves and murderers who had stolen his money and killed the woman, lost survivors like himself. But no living person had made himself seen. The dead were everywhere, lying in the street, slumped on the porches of homes, folded up in smashed cars. Nothing alive moved, other than himself. And that straggling dog he had first seen when he emerged from the hotel.

And during the afternoon another strange thing had occurred to him, a thought that quietly took shape and grew in his mind as he drove along the rubbled streets. The bombing hadn't been heavy. The few bomb craters that pockmarked the city hadn't been nearly enough to wipe out the population, hardly enough to account for the dead he found everywhere. The city may have panicked and fled, yes. Any American city, never before subjected to enemy fire, would quickly panic and run at the first few bombs. The city may have been hurriedly evacuated by the military, yes. But how to account for the large number of dead? There were bodies lying in streets that contained no craters, no evidence of war at all.

'Holy Mother of Moses! Gas!' And then he paused. No, not gas. Gas would have found him in his third floor room unless it were some strange new kind that clung to the surface, did not rise. He stooped and sniffed the street, the grass growing on the lawns. There was no odour of gas. And that dog was still alive. Not gas then. What?

Atomic radiation? Bacterial bombs? He didn't know; he knew nothing about them. He knew as much about them as any other G.I. did, which was next to nothing. But those craters could have been made by special, hellish bombs that killed without steel splinters, without shrapnel. It could account for those lifeless bodies lying far from the craters, could account for the dead and deserted city. How did you go about looking for radiation? Oh yes – Geiger counters.

Gary didn't have a counter, wouldn't know where they could be found, wouldn't know how to use one if he had it. Bacteria? Germs of some kind. You can't fight germs. If his induction shots didn't protect him, to hell with it.

He was still alive. So he was immune to whatever hit the

city, or the stuff didn't reach to the third floor. He was still alive in a city of the dead.

The jarring crash of a plate glass window brought him to his feet. Someone *else* was alive.

The sound had come from somewhere off to his left, surprisingly near, and after a moment of frozen surprise and indecision, he leaped for the car. A following thought stopped him. The sound of the motor might scare them away, might scare them – whoever they were – into hiding. He turned from the car and ran lightly up the street, swinging his eyes from side to side. Broken glass lay everywhere and it was impossible to determine which window had been breached. He slowed, trotted cautiously, eyes and ears alert.

He came to a cross street, peered up and down its length without seeing anything, and crossed over to continue his route. The darkness of evening was closing in. Slowly now he paced along the street, avoiding the glass that might crunch underfoot and betray him, side-stepping the rubble that barred his way. He hurried along to the next cross street, and the next after that, until he felt that he had come too far. It was like the house-to-house searches in those bombed-out French towns – you sometimes sensed the presence of humans and again you knew beforehand that a house was empty. He realised now, with a surprising return of that old sense, that he had passed the person who smashed the window.

Gary turned and retraced his route, cautiously.

He spotted the brief flicker of a flashlight ahead of him and dropped to the street, studying the building as he approached it. Quite apparently a jewellery shop. Looters then – but the whole city lay open for the taking. What was the especial crime of this one act? In a sense he had looted a grocery and a clothing store himself. Somebody wanted the valuable stuff.

The light flicked on again, scanning a row of display cases along one wall. He caught a faint silhouette created by the small light. He crept nearer, was rising to his feet when he heard the joyous exclamation.

The looter was a woman.

Gary sank back to the pavement, thinking better of rushing her. The woman on the hotel's third floor had been murdered by a thief; this feminine looter could be well armed. She might misinterpret his approach and shoot him. He had no desire to stop her, to prevent her from taking what she wanted. He was interested only in her, not in what she was doing. She was the only living thing he had found in the town except for the dog, and the dog wouldn't make good company. He stayed in the street, waiting.

The woman in the shop took her time, picking over the stock, obviously enjoying herself. Once or twice she flicked off the light and stepped to the broken window, searching the street for people. Gary was only another shapeless bundle of nothing on the black street. She did not see him. He heard the tinkle of gems and rings as she gathered them up in a bundle.

When she had satisfied herself and at last came out of the shop she was carrying a brown paper sack stuffed with loot. She briefly switched on the light to find her footing and left the store as she had entered, through the gaping hole knocked in the heavy window. Gary tensed his muscles and waited. She turned towards him. Holding the sack clutched tightly in one hand and the flash in the other, she made her way along the street as he had done, avoiding the rubble. Accepting his flattened body as just another obstacle, she was steering a course around him when he leaped.

The woman screamed in terror and struck out with the flashlight. He knocked it from her hand and shoved her backwards, crooking one foot behind her legs as she stumbled. She fell back, sprawling and screaming, the paper sack bursting as it hit the pavement.

He was on her in an instant, pinning her down, trying vainly to clamp a hand over her mouth to throttle the screams.

'Shut up!' he shouted. He got a palm over her mouth and she bit him. 'Shut up – I won't hurt you!'

'You're a cop . . . ' Her voice was girlish and shrill with terror. 'You're a cop!'

'I'm not a cop. Dammit, shut up. *Shut up!*'

He caught a piece of cloth from her dress collar and stuffed it in her mouth, holding it down with his hand. The screams were cut short. She tried to kick but he threw his legs over hers, holding her to the ground. A hand came up and pointed fingernails raked his cheek agonisingly. He slapped her then, slapped her sharply and with force across the face. She went limp. He didn't relax his grip but cautiously kept her pinned down, alert for any trick. In the uncertain darkness her body seemed small and frail.

When he saw she was choking, he pulled the gag from her mouth to discover she was crying.

'Oh hell, shut that up! That's worse than screaming.'

'Take it, take it,' she shrilled at him. 'I can't stop you. Take it and leave me alone!'

'Stop it, will you? Listen to me. I'm not going to hurt you.'

The crying continued. 'You're a cop.'

'I'm not a cop but if you don't stop that damned blubbering I'll make you wish I was.' He balled a fist and pushed it into her face, shoved it so close to her eyes that she couldn't mistake it even in the darkness. 'Stop it – *now*.'

She stopped. The stopping was drawn out like a motor choked off with a fouled feed line, but she stopped. He rolled off her body and sat up to watch her.

She made no move, simply lay there in the street staring up at his dark shape against the sky. The silence of the street and the city fell around them.

'What do you want?' she asked finally.

'You.'

'I can't stop you,' she threw back sarcastically.

'Don't act stupid *You.*' He thrust a pointed finger at her shoulder. 'You're alive – you're the only one left alive in this man's town. You're alive and I'm alive. Does that make sense to you?'

'I suppose so.' Her voice was small, far-away.

Acting on a sudden suspicion, he groped around in the street for the flashlight, found it and put the beam on her face. The face was white with the last lingering traces of her fright, her eyes wide and brilliant blue in the darkness. She flinched under the probing beam.

'Mother of Moses – you're just a kid!'

'I'm not,' she snapped. 'I'm nineteen.'

'You're a liar. You're just a kid, fifteen or sixteen maybe.'

'I'm nineteen,' she insisted. 'I can prove it.'

'How?' he asked sceptically, dousing the flash.

'I'm in college – a junior.'

'That doesn't mean a thing to me.' He stared along the street, alert for any movement in the night. Turning over her answer, he admitted grudgingly: 'Well, maybe seventeen.'

'Nineteen,' she still insisted.

'Skip it.' He got to his knees. 'Are you going to behave? What's your name?'

'Irma. Irma Sloane. What's yours?'

'Call me Gary. Are you going to behave now?'

'Gary what?'

'Russell Gary. Answer me.'

'All right, don't get mad.' She sat up, felt around on the pavement for the scattered jewellery. 'Look what you made me do!' Abruptly she was on her knees and frantically searching the street. 'Help me find them. I want them, I want them all. Help me!'

He held the light for her, contemptuously watching and sweeping it around in ever widening circles as she scrabbled over the street gathering up the spilled loot. When she had recovered all that could be found in the light's dim beam, she brought the double handful of gems over to dump them in his trouser pockets.

'We'll have to come back here tomorrow. I know I've missed some.'

'To hell with that,' he told her. 'There's other stores around here.'

'Yes!' She paused in pleased surprise. 'That's right. There are many of them; I know where they all are. We'll find them tomorrow, you and I.'

He contradicted her. 'We'll get the devil out of here tomorrow, and fast. Don't you know what this city will be like this time tomorrow night?'

'But Russell, my jewellery – What will it be like?'

'What do you think, with those bodies under two or three days of baking sun?'

'Oh . . . ' She was silent, and took the flashlight from his hand to direct the beam up into his face. He squinted against the sudden light and heard her indrawn breath.

'What's the matter?'

'Nothing, Russell. But you need a shave.'

He took the light from her hand and shut it off. 'Let's get away from here.'

'Where are we going?'

He hesitated. Where were they going?

They stood like silent sentinels in the middle of a dead, deserted city, an odorous city lying lifeless under a black night sky – the victim of some enemy's bombs. They alone, for all he knew, among uncounted dead. They and a stray dog. Where to go? Certainly not back to that place where he had spent the previous nights. Were it not for the girl he knew what he would have preferred, what he would have done. A pair of blankets from the first shop offering such merchandise, and a bunk in the fields outside of town, out of reach of the smell and reminder of death. Or a vacant farmhouse whose occupants had left before disaster struck.

She put a small hand in his, anxiously waiting.

'Do you live here?' he asked. 'Do you know the town?'

'I've lived here all my life. I know it all.'

'Find us a hotel,' he directed then, 'a big one.'

She hesitated only a moment and he could guess what she might be thinking. 'Where are we now?' she asked him.

They picked their way to the nearest intersection and he turned the light on the street sign.

'Oh, yes,' she said then. 'This way.'

The lobby seemed empty. He searched it carefully in the beam of the flashlight before advancing across it. The desk clerk was slumped on the floor behind his desk.

'This bombing,' Gary said, 'did it come at night?'

'The bom – oh, yes. In the early evening. The radio said some planes had been shot down, and something about long-range rockets. It wasn't very clear.'

He went behind the clerk's desk and scanned the key rack, finally taking several of them from their slots. 'How did you escape. Where were you?'

'Oh, I wasn't here. I was with my class in Havana. Do you know where that is?'

'No.'

'A small town south of here; my class was on an archaeological field trip. There are Indian mounds at Havana.'

'Still sticking to your story?'

'I *am* nineteen!' she declared with anger.

'I won't argue about it; I don't give a damn how old you are. Come on.' He walked to the stairs. 'What happened to the rest of the class?'

'I don't know. When we heard the news on the radio, I came home. Home was . . . home was . . . '

'Bombed out?' He led her up the stairway.

'No. It hadn't been touched. But inside, Mother was . . . dead. Her body had turned colour, sort of purple.'

'Purple?'

'Bluish-purple. I can't describe it. It was ugly.'

'I can't figure that one out. Some disease? It worked fast, damned fast. Say – when did this happen, this bombing? Wednesday night?'

'I think so. Yes, Wednesday evening.'

'And this is Friday.' He shook his head.

They continued to climb the carpeted stairs. At the second floor landing he paused only long enough to send the light flashing down the corridor, to assure himself that it was empty, and started upwards again, pulling the girl along. He believed the third or the fourth floor would be the safest, away from the street. The silent city might contain other prowlers besides themselves.

'What have you been doing since Wednesday night?'

'I don't know. Honestly I don't.' She shuddered. 'I came home and found – It was unpleasant. I cried a lot, and I was sick. Every time I attempted to eat I was sick. I guess I've lived on canned juices, and soup. There was no electricity, no running water.'

'Power station must be out,' he explained. 'Either a bomb struck it or something went wrong and the machinery shut itself off. Automatic cutouts, things like that. Nobody was around to start it again. That explains the water, too. The pumping stations are run by electricity. I'm surprised the whole damned town isn't burning down.' He thought about her remarks on food. 'Soup?' he asked.

'The gas stove worked, after a fashion. The flame was very low.'

'Pressure giving out. It'll be gone in a day or so.'

'What will we do then?'

'We won't be here,' he assured her. 'We're getting out of this town tomorrow.'

'There's no place to go.'

When they reached the fourth floor he paused to examine the keys he carried in his hand, and then flicked the light along the door numbers. The keys directed them away from the stairway towards the rear of the building. The first room he unlocked and kicked open proved to be a narrow one, holding but a single bed; the following two were replicas of the first. On the next try a large room having a double bed stood revealed in the gleam, and adjoining that a similarly large room with twin beds. He pulled her inside, locked the hall door, unlocked the connecting door between the rooms and locked the remaining outside doorway of the other bedroom.

'This is where we bunk,' he told her.

She watched him, saying nothing.

He waggled his thumb at the connecting door. 'Which room do you want?'

Irma shook her head, not answering.

'Come on, kid, pick your room. I'm not robbing the cradle!' He put the flash down on the bureau top, still lit, and emptied his pockets of the stolen jewels. They made dim fires in the weak light. Belatedly he remembered to pull down the shades to prevent the light from betraying them. When he turned away from the windows she was still standing in the centre of the room, watching him. 'Which room?' he asked sharply.

'I'm frightened.'

'Not that frightened.'

'I'm afraid to sleep in another room.'

'To hell with that. I locked the doors.'

'I will not sleep in a separate room,' Irma declared. Her voice climbed with an hysterical note. 'This place is . . . is . . . *dead*!'

Russell Gary studied her youthful face briefly in the light of the torch, wondering what he was to do with her. He'd like to leave her, walk off and pretend he'd never found her, be rid of her . . . but he couldn't just abandon a child. In sudden decision he snapped off the light. 'Suit yourself. I'm taking the bed by the window.' And he sat down on it.

He undressed, taking off everything but the twin dog tags hanging round his neck. It was the way he usually slept; he hadn't even considered adding pyjamas to his wardrobe when he had helped himself in that clothing store during the afternoon. After long minutes spent in relaxing on the hotel sheets, he reached out to raise the shade and pry open the window a few inches.

There was the quiet sound of the girl moving on the opposite bed.

His mouth was dry with a consuming thirst and he got up in the darkness for water, only to remember there was none. Swearing, he climbed back into bed.

Irma laughed at him with unconcealed satisfaction.

'Now,' she said boastfully, 'am I nineteen?'

CHAPTER THREE

He awoke with the sun shining on his face, spilling through the open window he had raised the night before. The room was quiet and unmoving, a large and clean room in sharp contrast to that other squalid cell in which he had awakened the previous day. After a few moments the quiet and unmoving street below the window came to his attention, and he remembered where he was and what had happened to him. Nothing had happened to him – that was the surprising thing. He lived. He didn't move, didn't get up and rush to the window to see if the city had changed itself overnight, to see if the dead had returned to life and were moving about the streets in normal fashion. There would be no magical change, no overnight erasing of the nightmare that had killed a city. Yesterday and last night were too real, too much like those towns in Italy and France. This city was gone. His immediate concern was to find out how many others had died with it, how many others had fallen under enemy bombs.

That, and get back to the army.

Meanwhile, what would he do with the girl? Take her along and turn her over to the Red Cross – or walk out on her, leave her here in the city where she lived? He turned his inquiring eyes towards the other bed and found it empty.

Gary sat up, startled. Had she left him?

He stepped out of bed and padded across the rug in his bare feet, to pause before the bureau. The flashlight was still there but the stolen jewellery had gone. Turning, he quickly crossed the room to the outer door, tugged at the knob and found it locked. The key was not there. The girl had left him and locked the door from the outside, taking her loot with her. He stood at the door, thinking of her.

Nineteen . . . and she could prove it. Had proved it. He looked back at her rumpled bed and said aloud, 'Hell of a note!' And then he went into the bathroom.

The mirrored cabinet set in the wall was empty but for a few tiny bars of hotel soap and he slammed the lid shut in disgust. A dirty, bearded face stared back at him. The water taps above the sink still refused to run and he was on the point of turning to leave the room when his eyes found the water closet. Lifting off the porcelain lid and twisting the floating ball back out of the way, he scooped his hands into the box and washed his face. The water felt good on his skin and he poured handfuls over his head, letting it run down his body. A half dozen untouched towels hung nearby. As he was drying himself he caught sight of his beard in the mirror again, and stopped.

Gary quit the bathroom and walked to the door, forgetting it was locked until the knob resisted his hand. He muttered an impatient threat to the absent girl under his breath and crossed through the connecting doorway to the adjoining room, to let himself out into the hotel corridor. Going downstairs, he noted the room numbers nearest the lobby and on reaching the ground floor, scooped from the clerk's rack several keys to those rooms. Searching about the lobby he found a drugstore opening off it, and picked up a heavy chair to hurl through its locked door. The drugstore shelves offered him his choice of shaving equipment and he picked up a handful, taking the things up to the second floor and the nearer rooms.

The first room he unlocked was a sample room and he backed out of it, impatient at the minor delay. The next two rooms he opened contained bodies in the beds and he vacated them just as quickly. Finally locating an empty one, he closed the door and locked it with the bolt, to dump his supplies in the bathroom. Lifting off the lid of the water box, he used his hands to scoop out water and fill the sink. Then he shaved.

Afterward he lay down on the bed and ripped open a packet of cigarettes taken from the drugstore, smoking two in succession before the taste in his mouth satisfied him. It was then that he discovered he had forgotten to dress. Cursing his own forgetfulness, Gary swung off the bed and unlocked the door, to climb two flights of stairs to the fourth floor and his own room.

Both doors hung open – the one he had left open and the other that the girl had locked. He checked his stride and listened. Irma Sloane was inside, crying hysterically.

Gary paused in the doorway, saw her lying across his bed.

'Stop that bawling, dammit!' he said with a sharp and husky voice.

She swung around quickly, raised her head to stare at him, and then with a happy cry sped across the floor to throw herself at his chest. He caught her in self-defence, braced himself to prevent her lunge from pushing him backwards. Irma clung to him fiercely, still crying.

'Stop it, I said! *Stop it.*' He shook her.

'I thought you'd gone.' Her words were muffled, her mouth pressed against his chest. 'I thought you'd left me!' Her arms encircled his waist possessively.

'That's what I thought about you.'

She raised her face to his. 'What?'

'Where did you go?'

'Oh, Russell . . . you've shaved.'

'Where did you go? When I woke up you were gone.'

She smiled at him and turned her head to the bed, pointing. 'Look what I have. Oh, I have lots of pretty things.'

He saw the sack, an extra large grocery sack, its brown seams bulging with whatever was packed and crammed inside it. 'What is it?'

She released him then, straightened up from him and ran over to the bed, to dump the contents of the sack across the rumpled sheet. He stared half-believing at her loot.

'Mother of Moses! Why do you keep picking up that junk? You can't eat it.'

'They're mine! I'm going to keep them, keep them all!' She dipped her fingers into the pile of jewellery, letting the pieces trickle sensuously through her fingers. 'Aren't they pretty, Russell?'

'You can't eat them,' he repeated, 'and if you want to stay alive you had damned well better begin collecting food. Why didn't you bring something to eat?'

'I've never had so many nice things before . . . they are *so* pretty.' She looked up at him, and then at his body, to laugh gaily. 'Hadn't you better put some clothes on, Russell?'

He picked up his clothing from the floor and stalked into the adjoining room, slamming the door behind him.

They ate breakfast in the same manner in which he had eaten the night before: from cans, sitting on the kerb before a grocery store. It was less than satisfying. Afterwards he asked about cars. He wanted a new car from some dealer's showroom or garage, and he wanted a light one that did not consume too much fuel. She led him on a tour of car agencies and he picked a Studebaker sedan, a demonstrator with slightly under a thousand miles on its meter.

'Why are you so fussy?' she asked impatiently. 'Why not take one of those cars out in the street? There's no one here to stop us. Where are we going?'

'God only knows! We're getting out of this town fast but I don't know where we're going. Chicago? What if it has been bombed out? Supposing we have to go all the way to New York, or out to California? How much of the country has been bombed, do you know? Where will we find living people?'

'I don't know.' She was frightened now.

'I don't either, but we've got to look somewhere. The army or the Red Cross is somewhere and we want to find them. The whole damned country can't be dead!' He climbed in the car and started the motor, listening to it. 'I want a car that will give me mileage, I want provisions for a long haul, and then we're moving. Get in. Find a gun shop.'

'A gun shop?'

'Guns – rifles. Find me a store that sells them.'

'I don't know of any,' she told him helplessly.

'Sporting goods,' he snapped at her, 'big hardware store or a –'

'Oh, yes,' she interrupted. 'I know of a place where you can buy fishing equipment, boats, things like that.'

'That's what I want.' He drove the Studebaker out of the garage, listening to the performance of the motor.

While she stood absently watching him, Gary chose from the store's wall rack a heavy .30-30 and a Marlin .22. He loaded the girl down with ammunition for the two rifles, had her pack it on the rear floor of the car. Afterwards they drove by the grocery where they had taken two meals, to load the trunk with food. He stumbled over debris on the floor that hadn't been there when they visited the place for breakfast, and searched the store carefully before allowing the girl to enter. She would have chosen light, fancy and almost useless goods had not he vetoed the choices, instead filling her arms with canned soups and meats, a variety of vegetables, fruits and juices. On a second thought he picked up a case of canned milk.

She was quick to complain. 'Oh – Russell! Do we have to take all this now? Why can't we simply stop somewhere when we want to eat?'

'Lift your nose,' he said sharply. 'Smell the air. Do you want to come back into this stink every day to eat? And it'll get worse.'

Casting another look at the litter left on the floor by some other prowler, Gary drove back to the gun shop once more and picked up a .38 revolver.

'Now what's that for? You going to fight someone?'

He poked a finger at the bulging sack she held tightly in her lap. 'What if somebody takes the notion to loot *us*?'

'Oh.'

He left town quickly, picking up and following a marked route that he knew led to Chicago. Occasionally he was forced to detour around a blocked street where a falling bomb had gouged out a great crater, or a tangle of wrecked cars made passage difficult. The suburbs were less badly hit, with only an occasional crater revealing where some stray bomb had come down. But the suburbs were as lifeless. And still he didn't understand why, didn't comprehend why a few scattered bombs should so completely wipe out a population. Momentarily he switched on the car's radio, but the band was silent.

Either the army was continuing radio silence – or the entire nation was off the air permanently. Optimistically he told himself it was not the latter. Sudden and unexpected bombs had fallen a few days ago: more might come, or an enemy force might follow them to establish a bridgehead and dig in for counter-attack. In either event radio stations would remain off the air to prevent information from leaking to the enemy, to deny him radio beams on which to track more bombs, or his planes. The lack of information was harmful to the country, to what remained of it, but radio silence was of paramount importance. When the radios again came back on the air the danger would be over. He looked at his watch, mentally laying out an hourly schedule for listening.

'Look – look, there's a man!'

He slowed the car. 'Where?'

'There – that farmhouse ahead.'

Gary put his foot on the brake and one hand on the horn, pulling up sharp at the mouth of a lane leading up to a cluster of farm buildings.

'Hey there!' He leaned out of the window.

To his astonishment the farmer whirled and ran into the nearer barn, to emerge a moment later brandishing a double-barrelled shotgun. Immediately behind him the barn door ejected two boys, the taller of the two carrying another gun and wearing on his frightened face a stamp of determination.

The red-faced farmer waved his weapon. 'Git out of here!'

'Hey – now wait!' Gary shouted at him. 'All I want is information.'

'You ain't getting nothing here but buckshot. Now git!' He hoisted the shotgun into firing position, and beside him the older boy did likewise. 'I've had enough of you double-damned thieves!'

Gary slipped the idling motor into gear and poised for a quick getaway. 'Information,' he shouted once more. 'Where is the army?'

'Ain't seen no army!' And the shotgun blasted the air.

The Studebaker's rear tyres spun madly, throwing a shower of dirt and gravel into the air. Gary piloted it a fast mile down the highway before taking his foot from the gas, and then he slowed to a stop, to climb out and circle the car looking for damage. The buckshot had missed them. He settled behind the wheel to light a cigarette.

'Sort of mad, wasn't he?' he asked mildly.

'What in heaven's name was the matter with him?' She reached over and helped herself to a cigarette.

His answering laugh was bitter. 'You looters are giving us decent people a bad name.'

'Well, we certainly didn't get any information from him.'

'On the contrary,' Gary corrected her, 'we did. We learned that the countryside is already overrun with looters. That means people from the cities, the survivors running into the open country to get away from . . . well, from the city. That farmer has had so much food stolen from him he won't talk to anybody. Shoot first and answer questions afterwards.' He reached into the back seat for the revolver.

She watched him. 'You aren't going to –'

'I'm not going to what? Go back and fight it out with him? Don't be silly.' Methodically he opened a box of cartridges and loaded the revolver, to lay it on the floor between his feet. 'We also learned that people in the open country have survived; that was his family behind him. The bombs – and whatever death they carried – didn't fall here, didn't spread their gas or radiation or germs out here. Only the cities. Maybe only the big cities. We'll find out soon, when we come to some whistle stop.'

'What are we going to do? I mean – about this?'

He studied her childish face, dwelling on the almost mature mind that existed behind it, the almost mature body that existed below it. She had dumbfounded him last night.

'I'm going back to the army,' he told her, 'as soon as I can find it. I'm supposed to be there right now. I'm going to locate a command post somewhere and report in. And when that happens, they'll outfit me with clothing and equipment and ship me off to some place. That's the end of it.'

'But it isn't the end of it! What about me?'

'You? I can't take you along, Irma.'

She laughed at him again, an echo of last night's wild laughter which had burned his ears, made him ashamed of himself. 'I'm nineteen . . . and I could be a nice mascot.'

'Hell's fire, you'd have the army on its ear and I'd be in the guardhouse for life. If you want to do something, the Red Cross people could put you to work.'

'I don't want the Red Cross people,' she snapped at him peevishly, 'I want you.'

He flicked away his half-smoked cigarette. 'Tough, sister. The army saw me first.'

'Russell . . . ' She turned to him, easily forcing the tears into her eyes. 'Russell, supposing I'm in trouble?'

He eyed her silently, contemptuously.

'Well,' she wavered, 'I was only supposing . . . '

'You can get out and walk any time you want to, Irma.'

'I won't talk about it any more, Russell. I promise. Russell . . . will you really leave me?'

'I haven't any choice. When I meet up with the army, we say goodbye.'

She settled back in the seat as he started the car. 'All right, Russell.'

'We'll try Chicago first.'

They did not drive into Chicago. Gary drove near the metropolis, moving slowly and incredulously through the small fringe-area towns which infest every major highway leading into the city. He was turned back by the fire and smell of death borne on the night wind. The wind whipped the odour south, to where he finally stopped the car on the highway and got out to stare at the flames in the night sky. The fire had evidently been burning for days and now it was eating rapidly towards them, pushed on by the torrid winds. The unholy red glow of it stretched from one horizon to the other, indicative of methodical and widespread bombardment, making the city a vast crematorium. Chicago: bottleneck and major target, terminus of every railroad north of Saint Louis, possessor of the only waterway connecting the Great Lakes with the Mississippi and the Gulf, headquarters of a vast defensive ring designed to protect the nation from invasion from the north. Chicago: obsolete now in the strictest sense.

Gary clung to the car door and stared at the fiery spectacle in the sky, unable even to utter the curse on his tongue. It shocked him as that first city never had.

'Russell . . . ' the girl inched towards him on the seat, staring forward through the windscreen. 'Russell, isn't it dangerous? If atom bombs did that, isn't it dangerous for us to be here?'

He shook his head. 'I don't know. The radiation is supposed

to disappear after a few days . . . but I don't know. Mother of Moses! What they must have poured on that place!' He had read descriptions, had seen the army films of the destruction caused in Hiroshima and Nagasaki . . . and as he remembered it, something like sixty per cent of the cities were obliterated and over a hundred thousand had died in those two places. One bomb on each city. And Chicago with a population of almost four million had quite apparently received many direct hits.

'Let's leave, Russell. I'm afraid.'

He slowly turned the car around, staring first through the open window and then in the rear-vision mirror at the towering flames. Driving south again, away from the vanishing city, he couldn't help from turning his head to look behind. The glow persisted, hung in the sky after they had travelled many miles. It left him with a deep sense of despair that he could not shake off, plunged him into a mood and a silence so deep that the girl was forced to speak twice to make herself heard.

'Russell! I said, where shall we sleep?'

'I don't know. Anywhere.'

'We passed some motor courts.'

'I'm not turning around. Find another one.'

Sunrise the following morning was no better than the two previous dawns, no different from those other two unpleasant awakenings to a changed world. He rolled his head on the twisted pillow, trying to clear away the ghastly memory of the burning city. The image of the flames persisted and he found himself wondering if anything alive still moved in Chicago's streets, wondering what it would be like to be in their shoes. The picture would not erase itself. He had gone to sleep with the fire burning fitfully behind his eyelids, had dreamed of it, talked aloud of it in the night, and awakened in the morning with the red sky still fresh in his mind. It shouldn't be! Chicago was different from those cities in Europe, big and little cities that had undergone brutal destruction from the skies. Chicago was *ours* . . . and *our* cities were not meant to be touched. Chicago was not at all like those foreign towns that belonged to strangers.

Chicago hurt him.

He arose and dressed, ignoring the sleeping girl, to walk outside and scan the sky.

Gary turned the car west towards the Mississippi.

His reasoning was that the east was dead or deserted like the towns they had driven through, that the large cities crowding the eastern sections of the country must by now be only counterparts of the death and silence they found everywhere. Or else they were like Chicago. Deeper in the west there was more room, more space, and cities were greater distances apart. The place to find sane, living people, to find the army was somewhere in the west. He filled the petrol tank from an abandoned station and started.

The countryside they traversed was the same as the day before, the road and the few people unchanged from the previous unfriendly attitudes. Disaster had overtaken the nation and strangers were regarded with open suspicion. Occasionally Gary discovered an isolated farmer still working his fields, and more often a few men and boys hovering close to their farm buildings with shotguns very much in evidence. Some few farmhouses were silent with an air of desertion, while one had burned to the ground, smoking embers the only remaining trace of it. The small towns and villages along the highway were fast becoming islands of feudalism.

Some, like the farms, were empty, the population having gone elsewhere. Others only appeared to be empty as the automobile passed the length of the one, long main street. Gary saw signs of unfriendly people behind the curtained windows, the closed doors. Storekeepers were armed. And in one a heavily armed delegation met him at the village limits, stopped him. He explained his mission, his desired destination, and showed them the army identification tags hanging about his neck. After a while they allowed him to proceed through the village, one of the armed townsmen riding in the back seat to make certain they did not stop. The man had no news to offer, apparently knew no more of the general situation than Gary had already discovered for himself.

The airwaves remained dead.

In a town near the river he had his first piece of luck. Some country printer had issued a newspaper, a small and hastily assembled two-page journal turned out on a flat-bed press. The newspaper had cost him a half-dollar and an unending series of questions shot at him by the printer – questions which revealed the sources of the news stories in the sheet. With the radio silent, the mails unmoving and the wire services long dead, the printer had obtained his news from travellers such as they.

It wasn't much, and much of it wasn't news.

Chicago was treated in some detail because its nearness made it important and because a local family had attempted to reach it, seeking relatives. Every city of respectable size in that area had been bombed, bombed by some mysterious enemy – speculations all pointed at *one* enemy but no one knew for a certainty. The survivors of those cities were pillaging farms and towns and many of them had been shot. There were not many survivors – Chicago and Peoria had died under atomic bombs, but the other cities had been hit by something else, something unknown, like a gas that killed as it spread. Sometimes the survivors of *those* cities had wandered into the country to die later; they apparently carried the death with them, living a few days longer only because they were physically able to withstand the original treatment.

When he could, Gary put a question to the printer.

The old man stared at him. 'The army? Yeah, the army's out there.' He pointed westward. 'My son saw 'em.'

'Where?'

'T'other side of the river.'

'Thanks – I've got to get going.'

The old fellow shook his head. 'Can't get across.'

'No? Why not?'

'Blowed up the bridge.' He related the cold facts.

'I'll get across!'

He put the car in gear.

The bridge was a high steel structure arcing across the sky above Savannah, stretching from sheer rock cliffs on the Illinois side over to the Iowa shore. Its middle gaped and dangled openly above the river waters where an explosion had torn it apart. Gary stopped the car a quarter of a mile away because he could not force a path through the knot of cars clogging the highway, cars belonging to the group of seventy-five or a hundred people clustered at the nearer end, looking out across the river. He got out of the car and squinted his eyes against the sun, peering as they were, presently to discern a small group of soldiers milling around the Iowa terminal of the bridge.

Irma moved across the seat, slid out and stood beside him, clinging to his arm. She stared at the Iowa shore.

'Russell . . . ?'

'Yes.' It was an answer but she didn't recognise it as such. She moved to where she could watch his face.

'Russell . . . are you leaving me? Now?'

'Yes.' He pointed at the far soldiers. 'I belong over there.'

'Russell, you can't leave me.'

'Watch me,' he stated flatly.

'But Russell, what will I do?' She was frightened.

Gary brought his eyes away from the opposite shore. 'Irma, I don't care what you do. There's the car, take it. Can you shoot a gun? There's ammunition and food to last you awhile, there's that damned bag of glass you stole. Take it and go somewhere, anywhere, I don't care.' He raised his glance once more to the Iowa shore, squinting. 'I'm going over to the other side and get back in the army. I've been out of it four or five days too long.'

'I don't know what to do!' she wailed.

'Find yourself another man to sleep with,' he told her then, and shook off her restraining hand. 'You'll get along.' Deliberately he walked away from her, walked towards the knot of people standing at the bridge.

She let him go for about fifty feet. 'Russell.'

He turned his head towards her. 'Yes?'

'Goodbye, darling.'

'So long, nineteen. Take care of yourself.'

He approached the crowd at the bridge, worked his way through it to advance part way up the structure and stand with his hand shading his eyes, peering at Iowa land. The exploded hole in the centre was too wide to cross and he realised he would have to locate a boat of some kind. In the distance he saw someone observing him through field glasses, and waved at him. The wave was not returned. Gary shrugged, turned his back on Iowa to retreat to the highway.

He approached a browned, unshaven character who looked as if he might be a riverman, a man who leaned indolently on a car buffer and chewed tobacco. 'Any boats around here?' Gary asked him.

'Not now,' the man answered him.

'I've got to get across and get back to the army.'

'You a soldier?' the riverman shot at him.

'Yes.'

The oldster spat. 'Not a chance.'

'Not a chance of what? Where can I find a boat?'

The other raised a lean finger to point downstream. 'There goes the last one.' Gary's squinting eyes followed the finger but could see nothing on the river. The man spat again, raked him with an amused yet bitter glance. 'You can't get across. That feller didn't.'

'I don't see anyone. What fellow?'

'He's in that boat driftin' downstream. Tried to get across.'

'What happened to him? Mother of Moses, make sense, will you?'

'They shot him,' the riverman said.

Gary whirled to scan the river again but could not see any vessel on its surface. 'Who shot him? What for?'

'The soldiers over there shot him. He tried to get across, I told you.'

Gary stepped backwards a pace. 'Are you crazy?'

'I reckon somebody is.' The man straightened up and slowly searched through his pockets, to bring out a folded and creased sheet of pink paper. He handed it to Gary. 'Nobody gets across, mister. We're contaminated.'

The leaflet contained about two hundred words, a terse notice written in army doubletalk with some attempt to water it down for public consumption. It stated briefly that that part of the United States lying east of the Mississippi River was under strict quarantine, due to atomic and bacteriological bombing by the enemy, and therefore all traffic across the river was forbidden. It was hoped the quarantine could be lifted in a short while. The leaflet was signed by a Sixth Army commander; Gary knew the Sixth was headquartered on the west coast.

'Where'd you get this?' he demanded.

The other pointed a thumb across the river. 'Those fellers flew over in a plane and dropped them yesterday.' He turned bitter eyes at Iowa. 'Blowed up the bridge, too.'

'The plane?'

'Nope – them soldiers over there. They ain't letting nothing cross over – that feller that took my boat, he was a soldier too. Shot him.'

Gary read the leaflet again and stood there for long minutes watching the other end of the bridge, watching the soldiers clustered there. Presently his eyes picked out others patrolling the shore to the north and south of the bridge.

'Are they watching the whole damned river?'

The riverman nodded. 'Seems so. We're contaminated, mister.' He reached for the leaflet, folded it and returned it to his pocket, patted the pocket for security. Again his eyes sought the river, his lost boat floating away.

Gary turned his back on the bridge to face the crowd, to thread a path through their silent ranks. He found their faces dull, mirroring nothing but helplessness and unviolent anger at what the anonymous men across the river had done to them. The people gathered there waited, simply waited, hoping the army would do something about them. Their attitudes suggested they would wait until the bridge and the highway crumbled and fell away from beneath them, waiting for someone to help them. Gary cast one sullen glance backwards at a lone sentry prowling the opposite shore, and picked his way through parked cars to where he had left the Studebaker.

Irma and the car were gone.

He swore at her briefly, angry because she had waited so short a time, because she had taken with her the arms and ammunition he now needed. Picking his way through the cars he had felt a momentary foolishness at coming back to her again, a slight embarrassment as he pictured the sudden reunion, but these easily turned to anger when he discovered her absence. His first thought was to walk into town and hunt about for her or to find another car, but an idea stopped him. Glancing briefly at the people clustered on the bridge, he slid behind the wheel of the first car having a key in the ignition lock, turned it about and followed the road paralleling the river. There was no outcry behind him.

CHAPTER FOUR

Contamination and Quarantine

At the end of a week the phrase sounded like a curse, a vile term hurled at an enemy in the heat of anger. Pink leaflets were scattered by the tens of thousands in every town lying within a certain radius of the Mississippi, were thick like discoloured snow along the river highways and the blocked bridges.

Rock Island, Illinois, untouched by a single bomb and suffering from nothing more than fright, was sealed off from its sister city of Davenport across the river by army order. Contamination and quarantine. Rock Island looked across the one whole bridge spanning the river and stared into the loaded muzzle of an armed tank squatting in the roadway. Rock Island's fifty-five thousand population was fast becoming a special police problem because transportation had stopped and food was no longer moving in. Davenport, under martial law and supplied and controlled by the army, was almost its normal self. A tank waited on the bridge, facing east. Rock Island and the eastern third of the nation must wait out the quarantine.

At the end of a week some few radio stations were straggling back on to the air on both sides of the river, the surest sign that the military considered the danger of invasion to be over, to be averted or perhaps never attempted by the enemy. The types of bombing had made the possibility of an invasion a remote one for the contamination could strike friend and foe alike. In an isolated instance or two, in widely scattered interior towns, a voice on the air revealed that some life still existed there, some sort of electrical power had been harnessed despite the bombing. The lone voices haltingly took the air in search of news, aid, encouragement. Gary listened stonily to their broadcast appeals for help, their frantic quest for information about the rest of the country. He turned his eyes across the river and wondered if *they* were listening to the voices.

At the end of a week he had grown weary of listening to impassioned pleas and desperate arguments, to proposals and rejections between two cities facing each other across the dividing river.

And by the end of a week he had explored the state from the Wisconsin border south to the Kentucky fields across another river, to find the quarantine prevailed everywhere. He was trapped in Illinois unless he got away from the river, unless he drove eastward along the muddy Ohio searching for an undamaged bridge. The army engineers had methodically blown up all those structures which had escaped enemy destruction, all except a single span every few hundred miles along the river of demarcation; these remained intact but heavily guarded, intact for some purpose of their own. And everywhere they sowed pink leaflets, coldly explaining the necessity as they saw it, faintly hoping the quarantine might be lifted . . . some day.

Every day for a week Gary stopped someone, anyone, who might have a grain of information, who might know or guess at the nature of the catastrophe, without success. The guesses were wild and unreasonable and he rejected them, knowing from experience the cities had not undergone the fantastic poison gases said to be released by the falling bombs; realising by the application of common sense that the places he had lived in and passed through had not been doused by atomic radiation, mists, dusts. People and dogs still lived there, some people and dogs were still slowly dying there and his observations of the near-dead did not fit into any lesson he had learned. There had never been a mention of bodies turning purple, or purple as death came. Not from atomic radiation.

Finally he had caught a snatch of conversation on the air that led him to the answer. Rock Island was pleading for an open bridge, pleading its mounting distress, pointing out that pestilence and death had been spared the city. A brusque voice of authority in Davenport maintained a steadfast *no*, bluntly told the sealed city its fate was still to come. Travellers from the bombed cities were undoubtedly moving through Rock Island and those travellers were spreading the plague, sowing the deadly contamination as they moved.

'What plague?' Gary shouted aloud at the radio, and heard Rock Island echo his question with a dull passivity which belied knowledge.

The authoritative voice in Davenport answered in a tone of painful repetition, spoke of two distinct types which had been identified, added that only God knew how many others had been thrown at them. The voice repeated the names of the two, pneumonic plague and botulism, and passed on to the unswerving *no.* Gary listened for many minutes longer but there was no more mention of the diseases, no explanation of them. He switched off the radio and drove in a frenzy along the highway seeking someone who might have knowledge of the terms, stopping strangers at gun point if they would not stop otherwise, stopping armed men who patrolled their towns or farms, demanding answers of them.

They had no answer. And at the end of a week he found out another way.

He picked his way into Bloomington, avoiding the debris and wrecked cars filling the streets, detouring where the sight and smell of a body ahead threatened to turn his stomach, and cruised around and around the business district until he had located the public library. The heavy glass door had to be smashed in. He searched the long high rows of books with a growing impatience, finding nothing that might help him, and after an hour he climbed the stairs to the second floor to see what was stored there. The stairway opened on to an immense reading room heavy with a silence it had never known before, occupied now only by tables, racks of magazines and out-of-date newspapers. At his immediate right was an attendant's dusty desk and just behind the desk were the volumes he sought, an encyclopedia set. He shoved the desk aside and reached for them.

Botulism at first had no meaning as applied to the dead world outside the library door. Botulism was poisoning caused by eating food in which a bacterium had developed. Pneumonic plague was *see plague, pestilence, etc.* He threw down the heavy volume and reached for another only to find he had misjudged the alphabetical spacing, plague was in the discarded book. Plague was slowly giving him an answer when his impatient eyes skipped over the paragraphs of history and dropped to the bottom of the column. The reference there was *see also biological warfare.*

Gary abandoned the page he was reading and searched for another volume. That one, with occasional references to the first, provided the startling answer. He carried the tomes to a near-by table and spread them open.

Biological warfare began in a limited way during the war of 1914 when enemy agents were believed to have injected disease-producing germs into American cattle being shipped abroad. Biological warfare mushroomed into an expensive and heavily classified entity of its own in the war which began for America in December, 1941. During that war the United States poured more than fifty million dollars into new experiments for biological destruction, recruited some three thousand scientists to devise new ways to die. Both offensive and defensive weapons were produced, most important among the former being a poison, the toxin of botulism.

The toxin was successfully isolated in a pure crystalline form and methods were developed for producing it on a large scale. A really large scale wasn't necessary inasmuch as the poison was so deadly one-seventh of a microgram was a fatal dose when taken internally; one ounce was capable of slaughtering a hundred and eighty million people. The military machine thought to introduce this toxin into an enemy's food or water supply by agents, or by spraying from the sky. Unstated, but implied, was the definite possibility of its being introduced by long-range missiles, whether guided or in free flight.

Gary stopped reading, looked up to see sunlight through the windows. He reached for a cigarette, paused to inspect it critically and then put it in his mouth. The following sentence caught his eye: 'Among diseases suitable for biological warfare are pneumonic plague . . . ' He paused again, to reach for the other volume.

Pneumonic plague was a different kind of a killer. The plague was a dark left-over from the Middle Ages when

Bubonic swept a countryside and completely decimated a town. Pneumonic plague was so named because the lungs were the organs infected; the disease was freely transmitted by the spray from the mouths and lungs of other infected persons. The infection may spread – he turned the page – to other parts of the body, resulting in septicaemic plague. There followed a graphic description of the symptoms of the two, and the statement that one is about ninety-five per cent fatal whereas the other is almost invariably so. Time: death as early as the same day on which the symptoms first develop, or as late as two or three days afterwards. The final paragraph pulled his attention. The victims assume a deep blue or purple colour, typical of the last hours of all forms of plague, due to respiratory failure. The so-called 'black death'.

Gary puffed slowly on the cigarette, disliking the taste of it. His gaze wandered back to the brutal line of the other article.

Among diseases suitable for biological warfare are pneumonic plague, influenza, yellow fever, dengue, glanders . . . The United States, because of its particular geographic isolation, would be highly vulnerable to biological attack. Infectious diseases would be spread by air or other means and then freely allowed to propagate themselves; for instance, pneumonic plague, one of the most contagious and highly dangerous diseases known, could readily be spread in this manner.

Biological warfare can be a weapon as deadly and as devastating as an atomic bomb, in addition to having the advantage of being an inexpensive and efficient method of waging an undeclared war. A nation could be quickly and seriously disabled by subjecting its population to . . .

He flipped shut the volume and let the cigarette drop to the floor. Absently stepping on it, he slumped down in the chair and stared moodily through the window, unmoving and unconscious of the passage of time until the sun covered his face and struck his eyes.

So *that* was what was thrown at them.

Who threw it?

Someone to the east of them, the north and east; at least the bombardment appeared to have come from that direction. The north-eastern third of the nation was wrecked, pulverised and depopulated by bombs and flying missiles dropping out of the sky. Atomic bombs for the larger cities, pneumonic plague for the smaller, the toxin of botulism spread everywhere. Water supplies, the grain fields, wherever people gathered, ate and drank in sufficient number, someone to the north-east had knocked out the industrial potential and the greatest mass of the population. Quite apparently the bombing had not been carried into the West or even far into the Middle West for the Mississippi River marked the dividing line between the contaminated and the clean. The government had explained its present position coldly and clearly in the pink leaflets: the eastern third would be sealed off to protect the remainder. How much was left of the government, he wondered?

First Army, on Governors Island, New York, was charged with the over-all defence of the country. The fact that a western headquarters was now defending it bespoke the fate of Governors Island. Even Washington admitted what might befall it when it built secret bomb shelters under the Pentagon building, super-secret military and government chambers beneath the green rolling hills of Maryland and Virginia. Those chambers still might contain living people, but they too were quarantined on the wrong side of the river. He recalled that in the earlier war, the one which had swallowed him up ten years before, Hitler's underground retreat had not proved successful in the end.

Who threw it?

Someone to the north-east, someone whose missiles and bombs were concentrated on the eastern third of the nation for tactical and economic reasons. They could have easily originated in some spot as near as Greenland, an island almost as large as a continent and nine-tenths uninhabited. A source such as Greenland would not find it too difficult to shower death on those portions of Canada and the United States nearest it, with the West and the South escaping immediate devastation only to fall victim to pestilence shortly thereafter. The plague would spread as fast as frightened people ran. By now, he realised, it must have reached the southernmost tip of Florida and would quickly have gone to the Rockies if it were not for the river and the pink leaflets.

The sun reached his eyes and he left the chair.

He was immune. The past week had proved that. Therefore he could see no reason why he shouldn't cross the river and get back into uniform. If nothing else, the army offered him security, a precious security now that death in many forms stalked the countryside and food was becoming scarce. *This* food was contaminated and . . .

But he had already eaten it, and drunk the water.

Gary sat down again to puzzle it out, to think back to that morning when he woke up in the run-down hotel. What he had eaten had come from cans, liquids from sealed bottles. He had passed by the meats and vegetables, the bread in the stores because of mould and the decaying odours; he had not been able to brew coffee because water was not running from the taps. So he had opened cans and drunk from bottles. But what about shaving? *That* water was stale, clean but stale. It had lain untouched in the flush boxes since at least the day before the bombardment. And since then he had drunk only from bottles or fresh water country wells, forced to by the dry taps or the nearness of a well. The narrow margin between life and death, *his* life and death staggered him. Had water still been flowing from taps . . .

The only food that could still be regarded as safe, then, was stored on grocery shelves. And despite the immense loss of life, there still remained some thousands of people roaming the countryside between the river and the Atlantic. The grocery shelves would not supply them for ever and in the very near future an acute situation would arise. When the food began to disappear, a different kind of plague would grip the survivors.

A man would either be quick, or dead.

Gary intended to be quick even before the necessity of making such a choice confronted him. He quit the library abruptly, conscious of the several days he had wasted, and descended the stairway at a fast trot with the two volumes under his arm. Absently closing the smashed door behind him, he dumped the books on to the car seat and started the motor, straining to recall the location of the street which carried the highway through town. He stopped only once more in the silent city to pick up tobacco from the shelves of an outlying store, and then nosed the car south along the highway which would eventually lead him to the Kentucky border.

Briefly as he drove he thought about the girl, the nineteen-year-old Irma something . . . what did she say her name was? He wondered what had become of her in the week since he had last seen her, wondered what she had done since deserting him at the bombed bridge. Or since he had deserted her. Where was she now?

Night found him still rolling southward.

He cautiously refrained from using the road lights for fear their brilliant beams might attract shooting. The white concrete strip was not hard to see as it unrolled before him; he drove with only the dim parking lights aglow, to give warning to anyone who might be in his path. Far over on the horizon an unseen structure illuminated the night with its fiery, burning glow. Another farmhouse, he supposed.

Some time during the early morning hours he stopped for a few minutes to get out of the car, to stretch his legs and stand stiffly on the pavement examining the dawn stars. Waiting there, standing only half-awake in the very dead stillness of the waning night, he picked up the sound of another car coming towards him, heard the fast approaching whine of a motor in labour and the peculiar sound of hot tyres taking punishment on the cement roadway. Turning quickly, he discovered distant headlights probing the earth and sky.

Gary hesitated but a few indecisive seconds, and then leaped behind the wheel of his car to roll it forward across the road. He cut diagonally across the pavement to let the front wheels come to rest in a shallow ditch paralleling the highway, snapped off the motor and the lights and leaped out again, leaving one door hanging open as though the car had been abandoned. Recrossing the road, he sped back a hundred feet along the highway and dropped into the opposite ditch, to watch the approach of the strange car with his eyes barely above the rim of the depression.

It roared towards him through the night, making no attempt at caution or secrecy, the noise and the headlights magnified many times in the vacant stillness. When it was but half a mile distant he dropped forward into the bottom of the ditch, hiding his face to prevent its contrasting whiteness from betraying him. He followed the rapid progress of the car with his ears, judging its nearness by the overtaxed revolutions of the engine. It must be doing eighty or ninety miles an hour. He thought he could hear someone shouting or screaming above the noise of it.

It came rushing on, the reflected fan-glare of the headlights briefly illuminating the bottom of the ditch so that he saw his own outstretched hands before him. It was abreast of him, above him for a fraction of a second, and then it was gone, passing him and his ditched car as though both objects were non-existent. Carefully he raised his eyes to the rim of the shoulder, staring after the receding red splotches as they dwindled with distance. He stayed where he was, watching them until they were gone from sight, until the faraway beams of the headlamps had been lost in the night, until even the sounds of the motor and the tyres had dwindled into nothing. And then he climbed back on to the road.

Now why, he asked himself, had he done that? Was it caution born of long-ago battle training, or was it nothing more than fear of another moving car in the darkness? They had not been interested in his car, hadn't so much as slackened speed to look at it. Why, then, had he acted as he did?

He crossed over to his car and stood staring at it, still thinking of that other one. He could find no ready answer – but he realised he wanted to play the cautious role. Staring down at the rear of his car, he remembered the bright red tail-lights of that other, and without stopping to analyse the reasons for doing so, raised his foot to smash both red glasses and the small bulbs beneath them. Stepping forward to the dash, he pulled on the parking lights and again returned to the back bumper. There was no revealing gleam.

Gary jockeyed the car on to the pavement and once again drove south, towards Kentucky. He moved along slowly with the windows open so that he might hear the coming of another motor, drove with constant attention to the far road ahead and the rear-vision mirror, that he might see approaching lights while still some distance away. Only after sunrise did he leave the highway and pull up a dusty country road to catch a brief sleep.

The bridge spanning the Mississippi was intact, one of the very few the army had left that way. Two other bridges had been found and passed by as useless before he arrived at this whole one. And the opposite end of the intact structure was heavily guarded as always; this one was blocked by a big troop carrier parked sideways just beyond the middle, two soldiers manning a heavy machine-gun in the rear of the truck. Behind them, Gary saw an armed patrol waiting for something to happen. He intended to be the something.

He stopped his car near the bridge, got out of it and walked on to the span, warily watching the two men behind the machine-gun. When one of them moved, he came to a sudden halt. Unbuttoning his shirt, he lifted out the chain hanging around his neck and held the dogtags high in the air, knowing that he was making his point when the morning sun glistened on their metallic surfaces. One of the machine-gunners called to someone else behind him and presently a third soldier joined the pair stationed on the truck. The newcomer studied Gary briefly with field glasses and then climbed down again after a word to the gunner. Gary waited, knowing army procedure, knowing what that word was. After long minutes the third man reappeared, this time accompanied by an officer who wore a small white stripe painted on the fore of his helmet. Both men stood in the truck and put glasses to their eyes to observe him.

Gary righted one of his tags so that it might be read and held it between thumb and forefinger, hopefully watching the patrol. It was very doubtful that the field glasses were sufficiently powerful to pick out the small lettering at that distance, but still it was worth trying. Holding the tag aloft, he began a slow walk towards the centre of the span. Very quickly he saw the gesture was in vain and the movement an error. The officer half-turned to one of the watching riflemen, and Gary slammed his body to the bridge as that soldier lifted his carbine. Even as he fell he saw that it was no more than a warning – the carbine pointed at the sky and the single slug screamed through the summer air overhead. Gary scrambled backwards five yards before regaining his feet. When he stood up, he clenched his fist around the dogtags and shook that fist at the watching officer.

The officer made no reply.

Gary retreated to the automobile and sat down facing the bridge. Shortly thereafter the officer and the other man left the truck and the two machine-gunners returned to their perpetual watch of the bridge. Gary looked at them, felt a sudden resentment rising within him and cupped his hands to shout a single, descriptive word. The word had its beginning root in *muttonhead.*

'That goes for me too,' a quiet voice cut in.

Gary whirled, startled and alert. A tousled, unshaven soldier leaned against a bridge girder not far away. The man's uniform was in rags.

'Where the hell did you come from?' Gary demanded.

'The field over yonder' – he pointed with a lazy thumb. 'Was sleeping – until that shot woke me. Warm welcome, huh?'

'I'm going to get across this damned bridge if I have to break every one of their damned heads!'

'Sure. I said that, two–three days ago.'

Gary stared at him. 'Yeah?' He came to a decision. 'Sit down and take a load off your feet.'

'Was waiting for the invitation,' the soldier grinned. 'Some folks are touchy about company any more.' He crossed the roadway and sat down beside Gary. 'Anything to smoke?'

Gary passed him a package of cigarettes. 'Won't they let us come over?'

'Nope, not us, not even a general if he's on this side of the creek. Afraid we're carrying the plague. The lieutenant said as how he was sorry, but there it was.'

'The lieutenant said . . . He talked to you?'

'By flag. I'm in Signals – tore up some cloth and made myself some flags the other day. Had quite a conversation. The lieutenant's name is MacSneary, unless I missed a letter. Decent sort but inclined to be stuffy about orders. Mine is Jay Oliver.'

'I'm Gary,' Gary told him moodily, watching the two

machine-gunners. 'I was a corporal until a week ago. No way of getting over to the other side?'

'Not alive. MacSneary was quite positive about that. Pointed out to him that I was still alive and healthy – as well as hungry – but he answered that I could be carrying the plague even though I hadn't contracted it. Yet. Good sense, of course. Said that all of us still alive on this side of the creek were common carriers. He read that last in some army explanation and doesn't fully understand the implications, but it sounded weighty and he used it on me.'

Gary contemplated the machine-gun. 'There's some books in the car that explains it.'

'Am familiar with it,' Oliver told him. 'Was a science teacher until I was drafted.' He smiled at Gary. 'And that label is a catchall if there ever was one. Taught science in a small township high school in Indiana; biology, physics, chemistry, astronomy, was supposed to be familiar with them all. How to construct a wet cell battery, where Orion is located, on Tuesday dissect a frog, show the girls how to make their own cold creams on Wednesday, and since 1945 every succeeding class tinkered around with the theory of nuclear fission.' He smiled at some memory. 'Never did produce a bomb.'

'Ah, this is a hell of a note! Here we are supposed to be defending the country and they won't let us. What if we're invaded?'

'That, friend, is one worry we on this side of the creek will never have to face.' Oliver took another cigarette from the package. 'Our friends across the bridge may have a fight on their hands in the near future, but we're out of it. The enemy has made this section of the country so thoroughly untenable that even he can't land here, all of which leads me to believe no invasion was intended.' He paused to light the cigarette. 'Our lieutenant yonder is rather vague as to what happened – communications must be in a sad state when the army doesn't fully know what is going on. But the gist of it is that you-know-who unloaded on us. Long-range bombers, flying missiles, and apparently some fifth columnists who polluted the water supplies. They ran in a flock of bombers – the lieutenant doesn't know how many; but between the bombers and the rockets they pretty well blanketed every major city east of the creek here: atomic bombs and at least two types of disease. There may be more that haven't come to light yet – I should think they'd use anthrax on the cattle.' He waved his hand towards the land behind them. 'Shrewd tactical move – half the country done for and they lost only their bomber pilots.'

'I'd rather be on the other side,' Gary declared.

Oliver nodded. 'Likewise. Prefer to fight the enemy to fighting what's behind us – and will be behind us, shortly.'

'I had a supply,' Gary told him, following the thought. 'Guns, food, a good car. A kid ran away with it all.'

'Little buggers learn fast.'

'This one was a girl.'

'Oh.'

'She claimed she was nineteen,' Gary continued. 'Looked about sixteen, acted about sixteen the way she ran around picking up stuff. She acted nineteen . . . once.'

Oliver pulled slowly on the cigarette, watching the smoke. 'Would suggest we team up – if you don't mind company. Find us a truck and put away all we can. Stores'll be empty in another week, the idea of this is catching on fast.'

Gary stared at the patrol across the bridge. 'You don't think . . . ?'

Oliver shook his head. 'No. Been here three days. MacSneary said "no" three days ago and he told you "no" today. I've resigned myself to the idea of waiting out the quarantine – might be several weeks and then again it could be months. Would suggest you do the same.'

'A hell of a note!'

'Food is of the utmost importance. And guns. When these people begin starving they'll begin shooting.'

'Yeah.' Gary stood up and stretched, rubbed a hand across the stubble on his cheeks. 'Well, let's get moving. I'm hungry now.' He cast a look at the men behind the machine-guns, and again shook his fist at them, repeating the single descriptive word he had used earlier.

Oliver said, 'Likewise.'

They climbed into the near-by car and Gary turned it around, heading back along the blacktopped highway that slowly pulled away from the river and wound through flat, sticky bottomland on its route to the nearer hills. The heat was intense and the air not moving. His eyes kept returning to the rear-vision mirror, watching the bridge fading behind.

'The muttonheads!'

The machine-gunners blankly watched the car out of sight. A rifleman thought to replace the round he had fired. Silence settled over the bridge.

CHAPTER FIVE

Ex-Corporal Gary carefully stamped out the remains of the small cooking fire and with his shoe scraped a bit of loose dirt over the embers. The skillet he cleaned by scrubbing it with a handful of grass, and then turned it upside down to thump it on the ground. Finally he ran his tongue over teeth and gums to lick away any remaining taste of egg.

'That was the last one,' he announced.

'Pity,' Oliver said. Oliver was seated on a hillock twenty-five or thirty feet from the fire, a rifle lying in the crook of an arm. 'Maybe we shouldn't have killed the hen.'

'You wanted fried chicken, remember?'

Oliver closed his eyes, dreaming. 'I remember! She was a tough old bird but she was fine eating. So we were tired of eggs anyway.'

'Mention that to me this time next week.'

'Will do. Pity these farmers are so narrow-minded.'

Gary glanced down at his arm, ran his fingers along the frayed sleeve of his jacket where hastily fired buckshot had grazed him. 'Yeah. No respect for the United States Army.' He hugged his arms tightly about his chest as though to ward off the creeping chill, and turned his attention to the overcast skies. Behind the thick cloud blanket the sun had not yet surmounted the low range of mountains to the east. Around them the skimpy grove of trees was silent but for their few noises. 'This weather is ready to turn. We'd better be moving south.'

'These hills always snappy in the morning.'

'Snappy, he says.'

'How's the ammo?' Oliver wiped his mouth on his sleeve after emptying the contents of the tin cup down his throat. He shifted the rifle to the other arm and ran his eyes along the nearer range of hills. 'Enough?'

'Plenty. The damned mountains stay cold all day long.' He stacked his utensils in the skillet and pushed them aside. 'I say we get out of them and head south.'

'Willing. But we'd be safer staying around here. There were – and still may be – moonshiners in these hills the government agents never found. Did you know Daniel Boone opened up this country? Came through the Cumberland Gap and down into Kentucky; settlers followed him so fast Kentucky couldn't hold them all and they spilled over into Tennessee here.'

'Daniel Boone should see it now.'

Oliver shook his head. 'He wouldn't approve.'

'Look here,' Gary persisted, 'we can go down through Knoxville or Chattanooga – might be something there worth picking up. Everybody can't be bright like us and maybe they haven't thought about the warehouses, like that one in . . . Where was it?'

'Covington.'

'Yeah – Covington. That watchman was a crazy little dope; who the hell needs night watchmen these days with everything shot to hell anyway? Well – we should have thought of the warehouses before, and let the stores go hang. Small stuff. If they haven't found out about 'em in Knoxville or Chattanooga we can stock up where we're short.' He jerked around in pleased surprise. 'Say – Fort Oglethorpe is just outside of Chattanooga! I'd sure like to get my hands on an automatic rifle.'

Oliver ducked his head to peer intently through the trees. After a long moment he relaxed and swung around to grin down at Gary. 'What do you think the troops in Oglethorpe have been doing all this time?'

'Drinking Chattanooga dry for all I care. I'd like to make a stab at it. It's getting cold here.'

Oliver nodded and swung back to watch. 'Can take a look if you like. No risks, though.'

'I like my hide,' Gary retorted. 'I've hung on to it this far – most of it.' He gathered up his eating utensils and climbed the hill to retrieve Oliver's. Stacking them all together in a slipshod pile he walked over to where the mail truck was parked, half-hidden and neatly blending with the turning foliage. He tossed the gear into the back and closed the doors.

The mail truck had been an inspiration, a fairly new olive green job that did not blatantly advertise its presence when parked off the road, and having the added advantage of heavy steel construction, construction which fitted the government's specification to the manufacturer of 'armoured truck'. Gary stepped-up the armoured truck's mileage by adding a water-spray injector to the carburettor and pumping the tyres hard beyond their rated capacity. They transferred their stock of staples and ammunition from the farm truck they had been using, and took leave of the remnants of civilisation which clung to the river. The truck was not comfortable and rode hard, crawling through the hills at a snail's pace, but it offered a safety to themselves and their provisions otherwise lacking.

They had journeyed back to the river and that particular bridge twice, just twice. One visit each month.

Lieutenant MacSneary had not changed his mind during those eight weeks and on both trips the answer had been the same, with a pair of machine-gunners beside him to enforce the refusal. On that first trip back, Gary and Oliver had found a dozen or so people camped around this end of the structure, patiently prepared to wait out the quarantine. There had been a brief conversation across the length of the bridge with Oliver's ragged flags, and that was the end of it. Oliver ended it by flagging out a single word addressed to the officer, a word much loved and used by the army's rank and file. The officer stiffly turned his back.

The second final trip to that bridge had been far different. While still some distance away they saw that the refugee camp had been abandoned; closer inspection showed the abandonment had been in haste. Three bodies sprawled out on the steep span, bodies that while still alive had foolishly attempted a dash for the barricade. The machine-gunners had been faster. Oliver stepped out of the newly acquired mail truck and signalled his question, carefully avoiding the bodies with his eyes but unable to escape the stench of them. The answer was a curt *no*, and thereafter they refused to answer at all. Gary turned the truck around and started back.

'You should have asked them about our pay,' he said.

'Have a good idea what that answer would be.'

'Those boys ain't slow on the trigger.'

'No. I wonder what I'd do, in their place?'

When another four or five weeks had rolled by and the time arrived for the usual monthly trip, neither of them suggested the journey. With unspoken accord they thought it best to avoid the bridge. And so they remained in the hills, meeting no one, watching the woods slowly turn colour with the approach of autumn and the coming of cool nights, chilly dawns. When they could, they raided an occasional isolated farm or cultivated hillside patch, taking what could be stolen on the run. The hen and her few eggs had come from one of these.

More than three months had passed since the bombing.

Gary kicked each of the truck tyres with his foot, testing them, and carried a bottle of dirty water from a near-by pond to pour in the radiator. He didn't bother to check the gas, knowing it was low.

Flat on the side of the hillock, Oliver hissed against his teeth.

Gary snatched his rifle from the cab of the truck and hit the ground, rolling sideways to get away from the vehicle. He came to rest behind the trunk of a tree and looked up at Oliver. Oliver raised one finger and pointed to the west. Gary commenced a slow crawl over the ground, putting distance between himself and the ashes of the fire, circling around to the west to move completely away from camp. He waited to see who was coming.

A woman.

She walked towards them with no attempt at concealment, a very tall girl whose bare feet moved noiselessly and without effort over the ground, carrying her body with a peculiar grace. A thin girl with tanned face and blue eyes, who wore a faded cotton dress and uncombed hair. The dress had once been a shade of red or brown. Her legs and toughened feet were nearly a matching shade of brown, and sturdy despite her thinness. The girl paused a dozen yards from Oliver and stared at his rifle.

'Hello.'

Oliver nodded to her, searching behind her. 'Hello. Where did you come from?'

'Yonder.' The blue hills somewhere behind. 'Seen your smoke this morning.'

He twisted his head to survey the ashes.

'Did you, now?'

'Did. You hiding out?'

'Yes.' He glanced up into her face.

'Seen your smoke. You ought to use good wood.'

'I'm afraid I don't know very much about wood.'

'Guess not. I could show you.'

'You could? Now why would you do that? Why would you help me if I'm hiding out?'

The girl gravely stared at him. 'I'm hungry.'

Oliver nodded slowly, still watching the way she had come. 'Swap?'

'Sure, swap. I'm alone.'

With caution he raised up on his knees and peered over the hillock, searching the area behind her. 'How do I know I can trust you? How do I know you're alone?'

'I *said* I was alone.' She came a few steps nearer and stared down at his upturned face. 'I'm awful hungry. The other man can watch.'

'What other man?' he shot back.

She gestured off among the trees to her left. 'Him. I seen him first. I seen him when he jumped out of the truck.'

Oliver laughed loudly, sat back on the ground. 'Come on out, corporal, the girl scout spotted you.' He turned his head to watch Gary as he emerged from cover. 'The army could have used her.'

'Maybe we can,' Gary suggested. He stopped at a distance and spoke to the girl. 'All alone – where's your folks?'

'They died, long time back. Most everybody's dead. Folks, they went into town to see what was happening, and when they come back, they died. It's like the end of the world, ain't it?'

'For us,' Oliver said, 'for you and us it is the end of the world. The world is still turning across the creek, but the end has come on this side. Have you got a name?'

'Sally.'

'Welcome home, Sally.' He stood up and rubbed the stiffness from his knees, all the while looking at her legs. 'Take over, corporal. I'll fix her something to eat.'

She joined them as quietly as that.

That she intended to remain with them became evident after Jay Oliver had prepared her breakfast and then cleaned and stowed away the gear for a second time that morning. She ate everything he cooked, not speaking to either of them, but watching Oliver's movements with a curious intent interest. She had pointed out what to use for the fire that would not give off a betraying smoke, and then sat down cross-legged, feet tucked up beneath her, to let him feed her. Sally had not understated her hunger.

Gary was on the hill position as lookout.

In less than an hour they broke camp and once again locked the rear doors of the mail truck. Oliver climbed into the cab and took his place behind the wheel, resting the rifle on the edge of the seat near his left leg. He started the motor. Sally followed him into the truck then, leaping in with a quick movement to sit next to him, still without a word. Oliver turned to look at her, studied her face for an instant and then beat a short, sharp note on the horn.

Gary left his position and came running down the incline to the truck. He stopped, staring at Sally, one foot lifted to climb in.

'Company,' he said, looking at her thin body. His voice did not give evidence of being surprised.

'Seems that way.' Oliver was grinning in satisfaction.

'Your company,' Gary persisted.

'Been on a fifty-fifty basis so far,' Oliver answered. 'We get along better as a team.'

Gary hesitated but a second longer and then climbed into the cab and slammed the door. 'Suits me.' He shifted the weight of the rifle from his shoulder, resting the butt on the floorboards. 'Suits me.'

Oliver put the truck into motion and rolled it forward across the slope of the grassy hill, seeking the lonely dirt road which would lead them back to the highway. The seat was crowded with the three of them, their bodies tightly wedged together,

Silence held the cab until the truck had found and followed the twisty little road to the pavement, until they had turned south and were moving out of the hills for the flatter land of Georgia and Alabama. The sky remained cloudy and bleak.

After a while Oliver broke the silence. 'Me and the corporal are partners.'

The girl seemed puzzled.

Oliver correctly interpreted the expression. 'Gary – he's a corporal.'

'Army soldier?' Sally wanted to know curiously.

'That's our hero, complete with Purple Heart.' He broke off when he saw that he was adding to her confusion. 'Both soldiers,' he told her then, feeling her eyes on his face. 'Partners – we share everything.'

She didn't answer him immediately but concentrated on his face, studying his eyes and lips. The truck rumbled along the highway.

Sally said to Oliver, 'I like you.'

'Thank you – appreciate the compliment no end.' He briefly took his eyes from the road and flashed her a warm grin. 'I like you too – but that doesn't alter the terms of our partnership. The corporal and me: fifty-fifty.'

Sally thought about it. 'You want me to be nice to both of you?'

'That's right.' Oliver nodded. 'Or not at all.'

The long silence descended on the crowded cab once more. She turned her head sharply to study Gary, to examine his eyes and lips as though they were most important to her, as though they were the keys she sought to determine character. Their glances met and locked, each glance a neutral one that had not yet found time to form a bias. When the girl turned away to again concentrate on the driver's profile, Gary went back to his continual chore of watching the countryside for movement.

The mail truck rolled rapidly through some small, anonymous Tennessee town which appeared completely deserted. Each one of the few stores in the village had been looted and wrecked, the windows smashed and splintered doors left hanging on hinges. The body of a dog gathered flies on the porch.

And then they were out of the place, the last houses vanishing behind.

The sight and soundlessness of the town had reacted on the girl. 'All right,' she said suddenly. 'I can like both of you. Fifty-fifty.'

'Pleased to hear it,' Oliver commented. 'Partners.'

'But I like you best,' she added quickly.

It required several days to work their way south to the Gulf of Mexico, avoiding the larger cities and using only the less-travelled highways and sometimes a dusty country road. Occasionally they met, or even overtook and passed another automobile, but the occupants of both vehicles regarded each other with a maximum of suspicion and with weapons in readiness. There was no stopping, no seeking or exchanging of information. That stage of human curiosity seemed to have passed.

Sally was beside herself with surprise and delight when they came in sight of the sea, revealing without words that she had never seen an ocean before. The highway turned and ran parallel to the water.

The trio spent the mild winter months on a long, sparse sliver of land jutting out into the sometimes blue, sometimes green waters of the Gulf; it was a sandy island lying like an outstretched finger offshore from the mainland of western Florida and reached only by a wooden causeway. There were no signs of recent habitation. After Gary had trucked in supplies calculated to last through the winter, he and Oliver set about ripping up the planking of the causeway to prevent any other vehicle from following them. They hid the lumber in a ramshackle boathouse and lived in an adjoining fisherman's cabin.

The truck was parked on the seaward side of the cabin to conceal it from eyes on the mainland, and a part of the winter provisions taken inside. Not until several weeks of complete isolation had passed did Gary and Oliver abandon the habit of standing guard each night; occasionally the fast-moving roar of a speeding automobile could be heard along the highway paralleling the coast, but none ever stopped, none ever investigated their island. Vigilance slowly relaxed and a sense of half-security overcame them.

The cabin contained in addition to a small stove, one narrow bed which had been awarded to Sally without discussion, while they bunked on the ground beside it or sometimes out on the sandy beach. Sally, in complete if silent submission to the partnership agreement, was compliant with the wishes of both but as time went on she found herself favouring Oliver rather violently, and had some difficulty in concealing it.

Sally was lost in the enchantment of the sea, and enjoyed wading barelegged into the rolling surf with them while they fished. Fishing was a daily occurrence.

'That lieutenant . . . ' Oliver remarked once to the far horizon. He baited his hook and case the line into deep water.

'What about him?'

'Keep thinking of his precious bridge.'

'He can have it,' Gary retorted, wading in deeper. The white sandy slope of the beach continued underwater, forcing them to wade out fifty or seventy-five feet to reach a depth fit for fishing. The sea was clear and unruffled and so transparent Gary could see his feet dug in on the bottom. 'He's welcome to it. This is for me.'

'Unhappy position, though.' Oliver insisted. 'Wouldn't want to be in his shoes – suppose he had a family on the wrong side of the creek? What would you do in his place?'

'I'm damned if I know. Join 'em, I guess.' He tugged on his line thoughtfully. 'I don't like the idea of shooting up our side.'

Sally waded over to stand behind him, watching.

'Other hand,' Oliver argued, 'you wouldn't want to spread the plague to the western states either. Now would you? Unholy predicament the man finds himself in – feel for him, sort of. If you and I had started across that bridge he wouldn't have hesitated to shoot because his orders said to shoot. But lacking orders what would he have done? If his wife started across, what would he do? Or his kids? Can a man obey orders and shoot his wife and children? Matter would be squarely up to his conscience. Most difficult to answer.'

'Nuts, officers don't have them.'

'Officers do, but you can't see it. I don't think I'd like to watch the lieutenant make a decision like that.'

'I'll stick with this, thanks.' He turned and put his arm about Sally's waist. 'Just like a six-month leave.'

'Likewise.' Oliver stared absently at his sagging line and then again at the distant horizon, his thoughts presently returning to the bedevilled officer. 'I consider his present position untenable; couldn't hold it myself but have to admire his guts for staying. Wonder if he can hold out as long as a year?'

Gary was startled. 'You think this might last a whole year?'

'Not surprising.' Oliver tightened his line quickly, watching it intently for a moment before relaxing. 'Quite possible as a matter of fact. Keep us quarantined as long as there remains a shred of doubt – and that can be a long time.' He shifted his feet on the sandy bottom and turned to allow the sun to warm his chest and stomach. 'I'm not too impatient. Now if I were in their place – headquarters that is – I'd send patrols across all the bridges periodically to take samples and make tests. Send them far inland.'

'What for?' Gary asked. 'What tests?'

'Water, soil, grain, cattle if any are still to be found. Sample the swamps and the mountain ridges. Take specimens of paint peeling from buildings, almost any substance capable of concealing a foreign body.'

'Sometimes you sound like a schoolteacher.'

'Sometimes I do, yes. The patrols would gather up residue and test it for contamination; when the tested matter no longer revealed a danger, the crisis would be over except for mopping up the stragglers.'

'Except for – ' Gary jerked away from the girl. 'Like us?' he asked flatly.

'Like us,' Oliver nodded. 'Latent carriers, Typhoid Marys, apparently immune but spreading the death by merely breathing.'

'That's a hell of a note! Either they shoot us for crossing the bridge, or they shoot us for saying alive over here. What's the damned country coming to?' He jerked his line savagely through the water.

Sally left him to wade nearer the other man.

'May not be that bad at all,' Oliver pointed out mildly,

apparently unworried about his future. 'Not by the time they get around to us. All depends on the prevailing mood of high brass *and* the state of medicine on the day the bridges are reopened. If the stragglers can be cleansed and cured by some revolutionary medical means – welcome back to the United States. If not – why then, we're blocking reconstruction.'

'Yeah, fine! I can see me blocking reconstruction. Haven't they got anything to cure us?'

'Who can say? Science makes wonderful strides in some respects and yet stands still in others. We thought the atomic bomb would make the land uninhabitable for thousands of years, yet you can move right back in a short while after an airburst. When I was teaching school there were no known cleansing agents for the likes of you and me – and Sally.'

'What about that stuff I read in the library?'

'Oh, vaccines exist, yes, but they are intended as a preventative measure, not an antidote to be administered a year or more after the poison takes effect.' He was gazing at the point where the sea met the horizon. 'Seem to recall there were vaccines for one or two types of toxin of botulism, but antitoxins are useless at this late date. And as for the pneumonic plague! Perhaps, just perhaps, sulfadiazine and streptomycin could help if you were treated immediately.'

Sally spoke up. 'Is it bad, Jay?'

'About as bad as it can get, Sally. *Our* only hope is that medicine will find something new in the next year, something based perhaps on the existing vaccines.'

'But what about those tests?' Gary demanded. 'How can the patrols come over on our side and then get back without catching hell?' He had forgotten his line and was watching Oliver.

'Would use airtight suits. Something like those atomic radiation suits the bomb clean-up squads are supposed to wear. Set up a decontamination chamber on one end of the bridge and work from there; send out the patrols dressed in the suits to gather samples for laboratory tests, bring them back through the chamber and burn the suits if necessary. Easily done – standard laboratory measures. A series of such patrols would definitely establish when the danger was ended. If it ended.'

They returned to their fishing. Sally moved up close to Oliver and held on to his arm, watching the beginning of a small swell roll in and splash against her legs.

Neither of the fishermen had luck. After a while Gary worked away from the two and moved down the beach, slowly trolling and recasting his line but without success. Standing almost hip-deep in water he heard a car careering along the highway and was instantly alert, straining his ears to follow its passage. It was the first passing car they had noticed in almost a month. The car did not slow and presently the sound of it was lost to him as it sped rapidly westward. He turned and walked back to the couple, dragging the line carelessly behind.

'You know,' he suggested as he approached, 'there might be a way to get across the Mississippi.'

'Think so?'

'Sure. I saw something when we were hanging around those bridges – some of them at least. Did you notice the little signs down near the waterline? They were put there for boats to read. The signs said not to drop anchor there, it was a cable crossing. Those cables follow along the bottom of the river and come up somewhere on the other side. I could get me a breathing mask and crawl along a cable.'

Oliver didn't answer, still watching the sea.

'I could get across that way,' Gary insisted.

'Assuming that you evaded the sentries waiting on the other side, how long would you stay alive over there? How long could you remain free and undetected?'

'I can get lost damned quick!'

'You *couldn't* get lost – no matter how hard you tried. Dammit, corporal, didn't you listen to what I said? You'd leave a trail a blind man could follow.'

'Nuts. I'm immune.'

'Immunity isn't what you seem to think it is. And the people across the creek aren't immune. Your immunity wouldn't protect them, wouldn't save them from dying just because you walked by. Your immunity means that you and you alone are not subject to the diseases – at the present time. Just as Sally and I are temporarily protected. That's why the three of us are still alive. But Gary – your immunity may last you a lifetime, it usually does in common cases, and then again it may not. I hope to God you don't go across the creek, or under it. You'd only start *this* all over again.'

'All right . . . forget it.' He knew the wisest thing to do would be to turn the subject. 'Forget that I ever mentioned it. Let's knock off, they're not biting.'

'Wait a second,' Oliver said, and raised a hand to shade his eyes against the sun.

'What is it?' Gary followed his glance to see.

'Thought it was a sail. Couldn't be sure but for the last couple of hours I thought I could see a sail out there.'

Sally looked at him in surprise. 'There is.'

'Where? I wish *I* had a moonshiner's sharp eyes.'

'Over there.' She pointed to the southeast. 'It was there' – she indicated the west – 'and it went all the way across.'

'From New Orleans or Mobile, most likely,' Oliver guessed. 'Steering for some point down the peninsula.'

Gary couldn't see it and said nothing, dropping his eyes instead to watch the sea swirling about Sally's legs. The water rushed in with little waves to dash against her skin and form eddies about the parted legs, kicking up foam. He continued to watch with a quiet contemplation, letting the motion of the water and foam stir dream images in his mind.

'Oh, well,' Oliver said after a while, 'let's eat.'

Gary glanced up, startled from his reverie, to find Sally watching him with a patient knowledge.

They observed what they believed to be Christmas Day by going swimming in moderately cold water, and then spending the remainder of the afternoon on the warm beach sand. Sally lay between them, entranced as usual by the sound of the sea and the fantasy cloud-castles floating overhead. The routine was nothing out of the ordinary but there was no new thing to do, no new way to celebrate a holiday. Gary gave the girl a wooden link chain he had carved and saved for weeks, saved for the day, while Oliver contented himself by stretching out on the sands and resting his eyes on her body. He suspected Sally was gaining weight.

And at what they believed to be midnight of New Year's

Eve, Gary pushed open the cabin door and stepped into the darkness inside, to raise a pointed finger and shout, 'Bang!'

'Get the hell out of here!' Oliver cried from the darkness.

Gary laughed at him and backed out.

They made no real effort to tell time, to calculate the passing days or weeks, but waited with unspoken consent for the coming of a warmer season.

It may have been late January, or perhaps early February when the remainder of the provisions stacked in the mail truck were transferred to the cabin. The transfer represented the half-way point in their remaining supplies but the season was far advanced and they had no fear of the storehouse's being exhausted before spring. After the truck was emptied, Oliver tugged at Gary's sleeve and motioned him away from the cabin. They strode down the beach in silence.

'Spill it,' Gary suggested after a time. 'You've had something on your mind for days.'

'Bit difficult,' Oliver answered. He walked along with his eyes on the water, kicking up loose sand.

'First time I've ever seen you fumble with words. Come on, spill it. We're fifty-fifty, remember?'

'That's just it,' Oliver hesitated. 'About our partnership . . .'

Gary stopped walking. 'You want to break it up?'

'You guessed?'

'I guessed now, by the way you're acting. Why?'

Oliver turned to face him. 'Corporal, something's come up. I think it best that we break up.' He frowned and kicked sand again. 'Sally thinks so, too.'

'Spill it,' Gary ordered once more.

'Well . . . one of us is going to be a father.'

Gary held his silence, considering the news. It did not particularly surprise him, although he had not suspected it. He had formed the habit months earlier of taking Sally for granted, accepting her casually as no more than another woman, a convenient cook, a pleasant interlude. Now this new element had been added.

'One of us, huh?' he answered at last. 'How do you act when

this happens? Are we supposed to congratulate each other, or what?'

'I don't know,' Oliver said desperately. 'It never happened to me before! And I don't know which of us is the father – that upsets me. Sally doesn't know, either.'

The beginning of a grin appeared on Gary's lips.

Oliver was quick to stop it. 'I refuse to think of it in a humorous vein and I don't want any wisecracks! That's why I want to dissolve our partnership, corporal; right now, *today*. I want you to stop – '

'Oh the hell you do?'

'Corporal . . . ' He hesitated and then plunged forward into the most difficult part of it. '*I* want to be the father. Sally wants me . . . too.'

'You *want* to be? But I thought you said – '

'Don't play a dumb bastard! I *did* say it, and Sally *is*. You know what I mean. But both of us can't be the father, realise that – what'll the kid think? I want to be the father, corporal – the only one.'

Gary regarded his partner with a momentary silence. So this was the end of the line. 'All right,' he said. 'I can take a hint.'

Almost bashfully, Oliver put out his hand. 'Thanks, corporal.' He made no attempt to hide his relief or that he was pleased with the outcome. 'Damned white of you! Sally and I talked this thing over; we didn't know what to do. The kid scares her a little bit but the thought of you and me fighting scared her more. I'll tell her everything is fixed up.' He turned and started back towards the cabin, a wide grin pasted foolishly across his face. 'And corporal – if you're down this way next winter, drop in and see us, will you? Stop in and see my kid?'

'Now don't rush me,' Gary objected. 'I'll be around for a while yet.'

It had been a hollow, thoughtless promise. He left in less than a week, too aware of the sudden tension that sprang up between the girl and himself, and vaguely uncomfortable because of it. Both Sally and Oliver tried to pretend that nothing had changed, nothing was different and the old fifty-fifty partnership remained the bond between the trio. The pretending was false and the tension grew. Gary stayed away from the cabin as much as possible and seldom spoke to the girl.

'We've had some good times,' Oliver said reminiscently.

'Sure as hell have! I like to froze in those damned mountains, talking you into coming south.'

'Pretty good place to hide out.'

Gary loaded his pockets with ammunition and packed food in a shoulder bag, choosing a revolver and a heavy rifle for protection. At the final parting, he shook hands with a grinning Oliver and blew an empty kiss to the girl standing in the cabin door. She half-lifted her hand to return it, and then stopped herself.

'Where do you think you'll go?' Oliver asked.

'Dunno. Work my way over to the river,' Gary guessed with an indifferent shrug. 'Upstream, maybe.'

'No cable-crawling!'

'No cable-crawling,' Gary returned. 'Keep your eyes open.'

'Will do.' He nodded sombrely. 'You do the same.'

Turning his back on them, Gary left the island and made his way by hand across the partially dismantled causeway. Once past the opening where the timbers had been torn up, he shifted the bag of food to a more comfortable position and strode off towards the distant, empty highway. There entered his mind a brief memory of the girl – a pleasant memory. He didn't look back to fit the memory to the person.

The partnership was dissolved.

CHAPTER SIX

Gary hugged the blacker shadows along the shore and waited without emotion for the sound of the shot, for the sharp crack of a carbine. The doddering old woman had been a fool to believe she could sneak across the bridge, either she was starved to the point of sheer desperation or she was a fool. The darkness of the night couldn't hide her, not any more, not when the troops guarding the other end of the bridge were equipped with infra-red lamps and sniperscopes on their rifles.

This was the only bridge left intact along a six or seven hundred mile stretch of the Mississippi; he'd discovered that as he slowly worked his way north from New Orleans. Many of the spans that had been left open a year ago were now blown up, one more indication of the government's determination to maintain the barrier, to keep the quarantine. The troops now concentrated in strength at the western ends of the remaining bridges were hardened to their duty, almost calloused after a year of stopping the sneakers.

The old woman had no more chance of slipping across to the Iowa shore than a snowball in a cyclotron, not as much chance as ridding her body of the seeds of plague.

Gary crawled behind a concrete abutment and waited. He was careful not to expose his body on the roadway, not to cross over to the opposite side of the two-lane bridge. While he was too distant from the troops to be in any real danger, still some gun-happy soldier just might catch him in his 'scope and open fire. The old woman didn't know the army, didn't know their equipment as he did. In her foolish, hungry mind she might have thought she could cross over under the mantle of darkness. She *should* have known better, she should have known what quick death to expect after a year of it.

Or perhaps she no longer cared.

The old woman surely knew she couldn't live to reach the Iowa side – no one from the contaminated area crossed the river and lived for more than a few seconds, a few minutes. She must have known it and counted on it. She was one of the unlucky thousands still struggling for an existence east of the river, and she would remain there until she died. There was no other real choice, no other future. But sometimes the death on the bridge was much preferred to the death in what remained of a home.

The rifle cracked in the darkness. Good night, old woman.

Gary lay still, waiting. There was no other sound for long minutes. He knew the routine now, had watched it many times during the daylight hours on his slow, plodding trip upstream from the Gulf. Some soldier garbed in a white radiation suit would walk out on to the bridge while his mates covered him, move the old body with a toe of his boot, searching for a spark of life. If there was still movement he would put a pistol shot through her head. Finally he would pick up the body and hurl it over the guardrail. And then the man in the white suit would retire to a small brick building at the opposite foot of the bridge.

He seemed to hear a faint splash. The wind was in the wrong direction and he couldn't be sure, but the hungry old woman was undoubtedly floating downstream by now. She had reached out and secured what she must have wanted.

He crawled backward off the bridge approach and sought the sanctuary of a near-by field, cautiously seeking out the hollow depression where he had been lying when the old woman passed by a half-hour before. Nearing the spot, he stopped to listen and sniff the air, to satisfy himself no intruder had hidden there while he was away, Curiosity had made him follow the woman, the morbid curiosity of an onlooker who knows the game will end in disaster. She had been carrying no food, he saw that in his first swift scrutiny and again realised it when he became aware of her intentions. Had she been carrying anything to eat she wouldn't have attempted to cross the bridge, and he would have forcibly taken it from her.

The old and the lame lose their meagre rations to the quick and the young.

But her arms had been bare and there were no bulges to her pockets. So he had indifferently let her go on to the bridge, silently following for no real reason. Now he lay on his back in the unkempt field, studying the clouded, moonless sky. The night was hot and sticky with a high temperature, a typical midsummer night along a riverbank in Illinois. There would be rain eventually, if not tonight or tomorrow, then the following night. It didn't matter.

Nothing mattered except the real problems of living, the day-to-day existence. Where tomorrow's meals were to be found, the careful avoidance of armed men, how to live until the following day and the day after that. How to stay alive and reasonably healthy until the quarantine was lifted.

The army owed him a year's pay – maybe more. And sometime during the summer he had passed his thirty-first birthday; there was no knowing what particular day. But he remembered vividly the day of his thirtieth birthday, the day he had got blind drunk celebrating his ten years of service. He could have been among those lucky troops on the other side of the river, the safe side. *If* he hadn't tossed that big one. He could have been over there with them, continuously on the prowl, taking part in the river watch that never ended. And shooting at old women who tried to sneak across under cover of darkness, or who were damned sick and tired of quarantined starvation and *wanted* to commit suicide. He could have been dumping their bodies in the river, and waiting for the next ones. How long could he have kept at that?

His tenure on the beach at Salerno was five brief days but he hadn't wanted to stay there. The swing across France, sometimes at a run and sometimes at a crawl, was much better than Salerno but he hadn't wanted that either. No more than he had wanted the past year or thirteen months on the wrong side of the river. But – here he was and here he'd have to stay until the powers beyond saw fit to remove him, the same as at Salerno, the same at the Rhine. The one small difference to the predicament was that he had drunk himself into this one.

The awakening from that was vivid, too.

He remembered the dusty, lonely awakening, the firetrap of a hotel, the stabbed woman lying on the bed, the loss of his money and clothes. The bombed and deserted streets of cities had become a common sight but he still remembered that first one, the morning he awoke from the celebration. He had taken his meals on the sidewalk, eating from cans picked up in the grocery store. There had been the crash of a window – and that girl. The one who looted shops; now what in the hell *was* her name? Not Sally. Sally had been the winter in Florida and the dissolved partnership. Not Bea. Bea was the tiger-tempered three weeks in New Orleans before he struck out for the north. The name of the looter, then? The kid who laughed at him and proved herself nineteen? She –

A sound alerted him.

Gary rolled over on his stomach to bury his beard in the dirt. Slowly and with much care he brought up his rifle, muffling with his clothing the slipping of the safety so that it would make no answering sound in the night.

He peered into the night around him, straining to pick out a blacker shape moving against the darkness, listening for an incautious footfall or perhaps the odour of stale tobacco. A few near-by crickets continued to chirp, moderate assurance that he was still alone. The sound came again, between him and the river, and he aimed the rifle that way.

Presently he made out a moving mass not too far away, a mass that divided itself into three shapes as it approached. Three men, prowling the field. He followed them with the gun, drawing a bead on the nearest. They moved along in the night with a stealth born of practice but betraying themselves nonetheless because of their number. He waited. They did not stop, did not make the slightest attempt to inspect the field in which he lay hidden.

Gary relaxed slightly.

The three shadows moved closer to the bridge, slowing their steps too late to muffle the noise of movement, and as they reached the concrete abutment where he had lain earlier, they dropped to their hands and knees to become lost to his sight.

Gary lowered the rifle and began to breathe again. With that last movement he knew their purpose. The trio were scavengers, attracted by the sound of the shot from across the river; they came to the bridge in hopes the body had fallen on this side, or failing that, had left something behind worth salvaging or eating. After their short, fruitless search they would continue on their way.

He remained watchfully alert until they had gone.

A man, or a woman or a child for that matter, lived by his wits and his nature. The reversion had come fast in the year following the calamity. Whether that nature lay shallow or deeply buried, it had quickly come to the surface of every man who stayed alive. Wits were of the utmost importance, often marking the dividing line between those who lived and those who did not. On his journey up from the South during the spring and early summer months, Gary had noticed solitary plunderers raiding farmhouses, quietly and at great peril to themselves; and again he had watched a noisy, armed band burn another house to the ground and take what they wanted – at a cost of four or five lives in the mob.

Somewhere in Alabama a hulking, amiable Negro had shared a poor supper with him and warned him of some of the more dangerous coloured men to the immediate north. The Negro then tried to stab him while he slept. And also in Alabama he had stopped to watch a dozen women and children scouring the fields for grasshoppers, sweeping them into gunny-sacks they carried for the purpose. Those who couldn't obtain food by force or wile obtained it in another way.

In the hills along the Kentucky-Tennessee line he had discovered a squad of armed soldiers like himself, a half-dozen men who shared the common disaster of awakening on the wrong side of the river. Their leader, a private who possessed in brawn what he lacked in rank, had invited Gary to join them.

Gary refused. 'You're too much of a target – I heard you coming a mile away. And it's tougher to feed seven than six. Thanks, anyway.'

'Suit yourself, Jack,' the private told him. He stared at the tanned, well-fed body Gary had acquired on the beach. 'Where'd you winter?'

'Texas,' Gary answered promptly. 'Lots of cattle.'

'I'll keep it in mind. Hey – wait a minute, you can't get across to Texas!'

'No? Well maybe it was Arkansas – I'm not much good on geography.'

'Wise guy! Just don't ever cross us again, Jack, if you're packing grub. You don't get a second chance.'

'That goes double,' Gary replied. 'But I'll see you long before you spot me. If you've never been up in the line, soldier, put somebody in charge who has. You won't last long without scouts.'

He watched them out of sight, working their slow way over the hills to the east. The last man in the troop turned round to wave briefly at him before vanishing over a ridge. Later, Gary wondered if they complained to the private about their back pay.

Little good it would do any of them to complain, himself included – they'd probably never see it. The high brass would trot out some fancy excuse for not paying up – like A.W.O.L. And there would be a full year shot to hell. Thirteen or even fourteen months perhaps – it had been at least that long since the unforgettable day he had celebrated his thirtieth birthday. More than a full year for certain, for he had already spent most of *this* summer working his way northward.

He had no particular destination, nothing but a vague desire to see how far up the Mississippi he could go and still encounter troops. Someone he had met, someone coming downstream from the north had told him the river watch extended all the way to the Canadian border, and that after the river ended – or began rather, in a Minnesota lake – the troops patrolled overland to the border. The Canadian Mounties took over at that point but the risks and chances of slipping between *their* patrols were useless, for the United States had armed the border and the friendly nationals to the north were no longer permitted entry.

Gary squirmed on the hard ground and rested the rifle in the crook of his arm. The long, scraggly beard on his face was dirty and itched continually. He wondered again when the quarantine would be lifted. He had seen no exploratory patrols coming across the bridges as yet, testing and sampling as the schoolteacher had said they would. As far as he knew there had been nothing done to reunite the two halves of the country. The river spans remained closed and no one crossed to either side. There had been an occasional plane overhead but it did not attempt contact with anyone on the ground – reconnaissance, he guessed, photographing the towns and perhaps the people who stood in the open to watch it.

A full year now had passed, and perhaps even more.

A year. And in the dim beginning he and a thousand like him had supposed it might last a couple of days, perhaps a week or so. What blind and stupid fools they had been. The schoolteacher had been more of a pessimist in his opinions – his early thoughts were that the quarantine would last a month, even two. And now the first full year had passed and he was in the beginning months of another. How much longer would the cursed thing continue? Wasn't a year long enough to wear away the dangers? Wasn't a year much, much too long to be cut off from your own kind?

The damned brass was responsible.

The first few drops of rain fell on his upturned face and he waited to see if it were a false alarm, or the beginning of a shower. The rifle was snuggled under his coat to keep it dry. After a few hesitant minutes the rain began in earnest and Gary struggled up out of his earthy bed. Down near the river there were ragged trees and a hedge that would offer brief shelter from the sky.

He trudged across the field, soggy and dispirited.

CHAPTER SEVEN

Gary waited with beads of sweat standing out on his neck, knowing how near they were and not liking it. They were behind him and creeping in, moving slowly and without real nerve or daring because of what they were, but coming in nevertheless for he was alone and they were three. He hugged the bulky object between his knees and waited, tense.

'Don't move!'

Gary jerked himself up in simulated surprise and then held deathly still, waiting for the man behind the voice to reveal himself. The voice was not too unexpected – shrill, nervous, but still carrying a note of bravado because its owner held a gun at the seated man's back. The man would have two companions. There had to be three of them, although he hadn't been able to distinguish their number by the muted sounds of their slow approach. It had been a clumsy approach and he had followed it with ease, his back turned, his nerves tingling.

'Throw out that gun!'

Very carefully he tossed the rifle away from him. There must be three of them. He had spotted the three scavengers moving along the river during the day, parallel to his route, and he knew that with the coming of darkness they would remain in the vicinity of the bridge. He and they must have unknowingly followed or leapfrogged each other all the way upriver, from where he had first sighted them a week ago.

The nervous voice spoke again. 'Now stand up – easy.'

He did as he was ordered, climbing slowly to his feet and putting his hands in the air without being told. Instantly a pair of quick, fluttery hands was on his body searching for concealed weapons, for tobacco or food hidden in his pockets. This would be the second of the trio.

'I haven't got anything,' he said quietly.

'Shut up!' The bravado was stronger now that Gary was disarmed and at a physical disadvantage.

The hands went away from his body and the second voice became known. 'He's clean, Harry.'

There were shuffling footsteps to one side and a man slid into view carrying a shotgun. Gary looked at him briefly and recognised the scavenger, Harry. His glance dropped to the shotgun and he stiffened with interest.

'Now don't get no funny notions,' Harry warned him.

'That gun,' Gary said, 'I never saw one like that before. What is it?'

'None of your damned business.' The owner of the weapon motioned with its muzzle to the object on the ground. 'What's that?'

'None of your da – ' He cut it short as the gun came up on a line with his stomach. 'Diving gear,' he explained sulkily.

'What'cha got it for, anyhow?'

Gary hesitated long enough to sow the suspicion. 'I found it.'

'You're a liar!'

'Well – I picked it up back there a piece. In a store.'

'Step away from it – over there.'

Gary took a dozen careful steps to one side and turned to face the three of them. The other two stood there uselessly, equally nervous and apprehensive, watching him and their leader. All of them were in ragged clothing and all smelled offensive from long weeks or months without a bath. They appeared unarmed. The leader held the shotgun on Gary and made a motion with his thumb.

'Take a look at it, Sully.'

Sully trotted over to the gear and pawed it, not knowing what it was and therefore not knowing how to examine it with intelligence.

'It's clean, Harry,' was all that he could think to say.

'Spread it out!' Harry barked. 'Let's have a look.'

The scavenger spread it out, eagerly and clumsily, displaying the few pieces on the ground. Harry advanced and stood over it, looking down.

'Looks like a gas mask to me.'

'It's diving gear,' Gary said again.

'What'cha going to use it for?'

'I dunno – I just found it.' They did not believe him.

'Where?' Harry demanded. He kicked at it viciously with a ragged shoe. 'What kind of a store would have things like this? And stop lying!'

'I'm *not* lying. And don't kick it – you'll break the glass in the eyes.'

'I'll do any damn' thing I want with it, see kid?' He flourished the shotgun and delivered another kick. 'I'm boss around here. What kind of a store?'

'A place back there in town,' Gary said with ill-humour and jerked a vague thumb across his shoulder. 'A riverman's store – they sell boat supplies and things. They had that in the window and I took it.'

'Oh, you did? You was expecting poison gas, I suppose? If it's diving gear, what's it for?'

'I don't know,' Gary explained cautiously. 'They use it to go down to boats that are sunk, I guess.'

'It still looks like a gas mask to me.' Harry peered at him, bristling with suspicion and disbelief. 'Was you gonna investigate some sunken boats?'

'Of course not. I just brought it along.'

'You're a liar,' Harry repeated.

Gary didn't answer and the man with the gun lapsed into a disgruntled silence, unable to offer anything further. He kept the weapon trained in the general direction of the soldier's stomach and dropped to one knee, to examine the equipment. Harry tapped the glass eyepieces with a dirty finger and turned the gear over to finger the straps. Finally he picked up the heavy metal box fastened by a hose to the mouthpiece and shook it. It seemed solid.

One of the others crept nearer. 'Harry . . . '

'What?'

'I know, Harry, I know what he was gonna do.'

'Well, what?'

'He was gonna put it on and swim across!'

The leader shot a startled glance at Gary and then at his companion. He hefted the metal box in his hand. 'Not a chance,' he declared after a moment. 'They'd see him.'

'Underwater, Harry, underwater!' Sully danced around in his eagerness to please and tapped the box quickly. 'That's air in the box – you know, that condensed air stuff, what do they call it? The kid was gonna swim underwater, Harry.'

Harry lost his balance and sat down on the ground. The corporal stood quietly, watching him, seeing the idea take hold in the man's dulled imagination. Surprise mixed with a growing greed appeared on his face as he realised what the mask could mean.

'I'll be damned,' he said slowly. 'Now why didn't I think of that!'

'That's mine,' Gary spoke up quickly to drive the point home. 'You can't take – '

'I'll take any damn' thing I want, see kid? Ask these guys who's boss around here.' He got to his feet and advanced on Gary to ram the shotgun in his middle. 'Lied to me, didn't you? Figured on swimming across and didn't want me to know it, didn't you? I gotta notion to pull the trigger.'

Gary said hastily, 'I'll swap you for it, Harry. That's a good shotgun you've got there. We can make a deal.'

'We ain't making no deal, kid. I keep the gun *and* the mask.' He stepped back a pace. 'Sully, come here.'

The little man was at his side. 'Yeah, Harry?'

'Put that thing on.'

'*Me?*' Sully was aghast. 'Harry, I can't swim!'

'Who said you was gonna swim?' Harry shouted at him. 'Put it on – we gotta test it, don't we?'

Sully fumbled unhappily with the gear. 'I don't know how, Harry, I don't know how. I don't like this thing.'

'The kid'll show you.' He moved the shotgun. 'Go on, put it on him. And you'd better make it right.'

With open reluctance, Gary took the mask from the skinny man's fingers and slipped it over his head, adjusting the straps on his back and fastening the metal box at his waist. He pulled the fittings tight until the gear was snugly in place. Sully stood there, arms akimbo, looking goggle-eyed through the eye-pieces.

'Make him breathe.'

'I fixed it. He is breathing.'

Harry watched for a moment. 'All right – now down to the river.'

The four of them moved across the field and approached the river, Garry and Sully in the lead with the shotgun held to their backs. The third member of the trio trailed along without a word. The ground became soft and soggy near the stream and they floundered through it, Gary holding on to the skinny one's arms to keep him from falling. He hoped there were no prowlers about to overhear the noise they were making, for his weapons were hidden in the field behind him and the present safety of the four of them depended on the marksmanship of the man with the shotgun. He wanted to get back and get his own weapons before danger could find them. At the water's edge the party halted.

The river wasn't so wide at this point. Gary flung a glance towards the Minnesota shore but saw no patrolling sentries. They could hide themselves easily in the near-darkness.

'Lay down in the water,' Harry ordered.

Sully stared at him through the round glass eyes.

'Lay down!' He thumped the man's back and Sully fell on his stomach in the water, the muddy surface almost covering him. Harry planted a heavy boot in the middle of his back and pushed him under, holding him there for long minutes.

Gary waited impatiently to one side, alternately watching the man struggling in the water and the riverbank behind them. They were in an exposed and precarious position, easy prey to anyone who might sneak up on them, and the leader lacked the wits to post a guard. The third and remaining member of the gang stood uselessly a few yards away, watching Sully flailing his arms and legs in the stream.

Harry reached down and took hold of one of Sully's arms, yanking him up. Quickly he pulled the mask aside and examined the interior, as well as the man's red face.

'Are you all right?' he inquired of Sully.

Sully cringed, thoroughly wet and thoroughly miserable. 'I can't swim, I tell you, I can't swim. You was trying to drown me!'

Harry balled a fist on his face. 'Shut your damned mouth!

I wasn't trying to drown you, you dumb-bell – you didn't get your face wet, did you?'

Sully put dripping hands to his face in surprise. 'I . . . no.'

'All right. And you was breathing all the time, wasn't you?'

'Yeah, I guess so, Harry.'

'All right then, this thing works. You can swim underwater with it.'

'Not *me*, Harry, I can't swim. You ain't gonna make me swim under the river, Harry, you ain't!' He jumped away.

'Shut up – nobody said you was.' Harry turned to peer at the corporal with shrewd speculation. 'Thought you was pretty foxy, didn't you? Thought you was better'n the rest of us. Thought you'd sneak across underwater and leave the rest of us over here holding the bag. Well kid, you ain't as smart as old Harry is, 'cause *you're* the guy left behind. I'm just gonna take your fancy mask and you can go and find another'n.'

'But Harry – what'll we *do*?' he asked imploringly.

The leader stared at Sully contemptuously. 'You expect me to play nursemaid all your life?'

'But Harry – what'll we *do*?' he asked imploringly.

'Rot for all I care.' He reached for the man. 'Take off that stuff.' He yanked the straps over Sully's head with a rough eagerness and unhooked the belt holding the breathing apparatus. Sully did his best to help, glad to skin out of the gear. It was then that Harry collided head-on with his first problem. He stood there with one foot in the water, swinging the mask in one hand and clutching the shotgun in the other. Yet he needed both hands to don the gear.

Gary grinned at his predicament.

Harry hesitated for long seconds puzzling over the situation and finally made up his mind who to trust. He crooked a finger at the silent partner standing on the bank.

'C'mere.'

The other came down to him.

'Take the gun' – Harry handed it over – 'and keep it on that smart-aleck kid. If he makes one move, plug him.'

The partner nervously pointed the barrel at Gary.

Both hands free, Harry quickly pulled the mask over his face and wriggled into the short and tightened shoulder straps.

He buckled the belt about his waist and held himself still a moment to check his breathing and make certain the thing was working. Then, regaining his earlier air of bravado, he stoutly clapped the shoulder of the man holding the shotgun and turned to plunge into the water.

Sully took a few steps after him. 'Harry . . . '

Harry met his second problem squarely and lost.

He swam for a few yards beneath the water and paused for breath, unused to the exertion. Harry promptly bobbed to the surface and discovered himself slowly floating downstream. He faced himself upstream, unconsciously took a deep breath and went down again. This time he gained a few more yards before coming up, but this time he came up voluntarily because he couldn't see where he was going while underwater. As his head broke the surface he found himself staring at the three waiting on the bank. Burning with an impotent rage, he ceased swimming and promptly sank.

Gary laughed aloud. 'Hell of a poor swimmer, that Harry!'

Sully glanced at him in nervous fear while the other toyed uncertainly with the gun.

Harry finally bobbed up once more, downstream. He thrashed his way back to the bank and climbed out, shaking mud and water off the shoes he had neglected to take off. With savage force he ripped off the mask and let it dangle about his neck, to discover Gary laughing at him.

'What's so damned funny, wise guy?'

'You are,' Gary said. 'Might as well give it back to me – you'll never get across.'

'I'll be damned if I will! Maybe you think you could get across that damned river.'

'Yes – I could; I can swim it easy enough.'

'Well, you're not going to get a chance, not with *this* outfit, you ain't.' He walked closer and seized the shotgun again. 'Come on, let's move away from here. Somebody's apt to find us.'

Gary turned about with relief and headed for the comparative security of the field; he had been afraid the old fool would never realise the danger they were in. They had been exposed on the river far too long for comfort, a tempting target to a curious sentry across the stream or a predatory prowler on this side. He knew the raging Harry could not be relied upon to think fast enough or shoot straight enough in the event they were surprised; if the man were startled by something or someone in the night he was likely to blast away in any direction, heedless of the safety of his companions. The four men moved back through the soggy ground.

That shotgun was a powerful and deadly weapon, whatever make it was. He wanted it. Stripped of his own arms, Gary felt a deep sense of unease and emptiness based on the sure knowledge that the three scavengers would not protect him in case of trouble. He had to get that shotgun.

Upon reaching the field again he sank quickly to the ground and burrowed in, making his body as small a silhouette as possible. Harry followed clumsily and flopped down near him, muttering. Gary knew without looking that the man was fussing over the gear, forgetting to keep him covered with the gun. He clasped his hands behind his head and regarded the darkened sky overhead with a bland smile.

If Harry didn't discover the proper way to cross the river soon, he'd have to do a little prodding.

Twice more that September night Harry attempted to reach the Minnesota shore. On the second try he was spectacularly successful.

The first renewed attempt was a similar failure to that earlier fiasco and the man only floundered wildly in the water, unable to remain beneath the surface and never sure of his bearings. Too, he was making a racket that was undoubtedly heard across the river, as well as along the banks of the contaminated side. Gary remained alert for any other movement in the night, wanting no unexpected interruption to his plans. The always-silent third member of the band was holding the gun again but Gary was sure he could reach it in time if a prowler should discover their hiding-place in the field. Both scavengers were staring anxiously into the night after their would-be-escaping leader.

After the better part of an hour Harry came stumbling back, searching for them in the darkness. Wet, shaking with exertion and angry frustration, he fell to the ground and cursed the swimming gear, cursed his own physical shortcomings and the vagaries of the current which defeated him. Remembering Gary, he turned on him a florid flow of profanity, blaming him for first dangling a paradise before his eyes and then denying him the ability to reach it. Ignoring the manner in which he had come by the gear, he blamed Gary for deliberately setting a trap, and then taunting him with the unreachable bait. It was all his fault, everything was his fault.

Gary waited until the man had exhausted his foul vocabulary and his breath.

'Still want to make a swap?' he asked quietly.

'Shut your damned mouth.'

'Harry – listen to me. You've been running around like a fool all day; you've made enough noise to arouse every soldier on the other side and attract the attention of every thief on this side. If you weren't such a stupid jerk you'd have realised hours ago that I can't swim that current underwater any more than you can. Now think about that for a minute.'

Harry was incapable of that much thought. 'So what?' he asked instantly, weakly defiant.

'So I *know* how to get across without bucking the river and without making noise. If you had waited and watched me this afternoon, instead of jumping me, you'd have seen how I was going to do it. Now – do you want to swap?'

'Swap for what?' Harry muttered, half convinced.

'I want that shotgun. I'll tell you how to cross over.'

There was no immediate answer. Gary lay back and waited, counting on the greedy desire in the man. The silence of the night had fallen over the river and the surrounding fields, while somewhere far off a nightbird was crying. Gary absently wondered if it were a bird, or a prowler's signal. The two scavengers had crowded in close, listening to their heated conversation.

'How?' Harry said grudgingly.

'The shotgun,' the corporal calmly reminded him.

'Now wouldn't I be a blamed fool to give it to you *now*? You'd grab the mask and beat it.'

'I want the gun – it's a good one. I can go back to that store and get me another mask tomorrow.'

Harry shook his head, not realising the gesture was lost in the darkness. 'Nothing doing, I don't trust you that much.' He clutched the weapon tightly. 'And I don't give it up until you show me.'

'Then let your partner hold it,' Gary said savagely. 'Dammit, Harry, we can't sit here and argue all night. Let him hold it until you come back, if what I say is wrong. But if you *do* get across – if you're not back here by daylight, the gun is mine. That's my deal, take it or leave it.'

Harry accepted it after the proper examination for trickery and loopholes. There was little else he could do for reaching the other side of the river was the one and only ambition left in his life, his constant and only goal other than food to stay alive each day. What happened to his partners and the gun once he reached the other side was of no concern to him – so to hell with them.

'Okay,' he growled, 'spit it out.'

'The gun,' Gary reminded him again.

Harry passed it over to his voiceless partner. 'Give it to him in the morning, Jonesy, if I ain't back. Now come on, come on, I can't wait all night.'

Gary explained about the underwater cables, running from one shore to the other.

'How do you know them cables are there?' Harry demanded excitedly.

'I helped put 'em in,' Gary lied. 'I was working with the Western Union construction gang. The cables are there, all right. We put 'em in eight or ten years ago. Just look for the signboard – '

Harry was off like a flushed deer.

Sully quickly climbed to his feet and made as if to follow, only to totter a few steps and sink down again. The skinny old man sounded as though he were crying. The silent Jonesy fondled the shotgun and sighed. Harry's passage through the field was an incautiously noisy one; so eager was he to reach the bridge and the cables that he made no attempt to conceal himself or mask the sound of his movements.

Gary waited until the last hasty footfall had faded into

distant silence. He turned. 'All right, Jonesy, I'll take that shotgun now.'

The scavenger handed it over without a word.

More than an hour had passed since the over-eager Harry had shot out of sight, when the silent Jonesy spoke for the first time. 'Eh . . . kid?'

'What do you want?'

'I'd like to talk to you, if I may.'

'You're doing it.'

'You didn't fool me, young man. Poor Harry – yes, but not me.'

'Poor Harry is a damned fool,' Gary retorted. He lay outstretched on his belly, chin buried in the dirt and the treasured shotgun cradled in his arms. Gary's senses were alert, his eyes and ears directed towards the distant river. 'So?'

'I have watched you, of course, since we came upon you. Army, weren't you – or perhaps the Marines? You could have jumped Harry a dozen times today – there were plenty of opportunities. And you could have taken the gun away from me any time you wished. But you didn't, you deliberately held off. Why?'

'I wanted Harry – or somebody – to tackle the river,' the corporal answered.

'I realise that. I realised what you were trying to do when you introduced the marine gear and yet passed up an opportunity to seize the gun. But why? Why didn't you swim across and let us go hang?'

Gary grinned and the macabre humour of it was reflected in his voice. 'I'm no test pilot, Jonesy. I think up the ideas and let somebody else try them out. If Harry makes it, I can – later on and at another bridge.'

'And if he doesn't?'

'Then I'll know the soldier boys over there are wise to *that* angle, too. And I'll have to figure out another way.'

'I see,' Jonesy said and lapsed into silence.

'This gun,' Gary said after a while, 'where did he get it?'

'From my store.'

'Your store?'

'A sporting goods store where I worked before the . . . the disaster. Near here, so to speak. Harry wanted a good shotgun and I selected that one for him.'

'Where's yours?'

'I don't have one – Harry wouldn't permit it. And I've never fired a shot in my life.'

A short distance away the thin old man lay on the ground, openly weeping and oblivious to those around him.

Gary asked in annoyance, 'What's the matter with him?'

'Scared, lonely, lost. He is Harry's father.' The former merchant paused in speculation. 'I suppose I'll have to look after him if Harry doesn't come back.'

Gary fingered the stock of the shotgun, tracing it with his fingertips. 'This is a new one on me. What is it?'

'The gun? A Browning Automatic, one of the best of my stock. You'll find it an excellent weapon: full choke and the very best steel, the magazine holds five shells in addition to a sixth in the chamber. The retail price is a hundred and twelve dollars.'

'Knock it off, I'm not going to buy it. Got shells?'

'Yes, quite a few. In Harry's bag, there . . . '

'Thanks,' Gary said dryly.

'I'd like to ask one more question if I may?'

'What?'

'This afternoon when we came upon you sitting there in the field, fussing with the underwater apparatus . . . eh, you *knew* we were behind you, didn't you?'

'Heard you coming a mile away.'

'I rather thought so,' Jonesy commented. 'While you acted as though you had been taken by surprise, still – ' He broke off, startled out of his wits as the night sky lit up with a burning incandescence. The night was bright and white around them, reflecting the varied emotions on their faces. 'Good God! What's that?' Jonesy sat up.

Gary froze to the ground, unmoving, searching the field with narrowed eyes. Both Jonesy and the old man were stiffly upright, staring at the brilliant light in the sky.

'Hit the dirt, you damned fool!' Gary snapped.

The darkness was split with light and sound.

A rifle cracked suddenly on the other side of the river, half a mile to the south of the field where they lay hidden. A heart-beat later the first machine-gun cut loose to shatter the night with its rapid song, followed instantly by another. Gary listened to the guns, recognising their make and calibre by memory. There came a flurry of whistles and the guns stopped firing. In the new silence a belated rifle spoke once and was still. Very slowly the hanging light faded from the sky and night took over its rightful domain.

'*What was that?*' Jonesy demanded again in a shaking, frightened voice. The older man had sidled near him.

'That was your friend Harry,' the corporal answered. 'He made it all right.'

'They . . . they killed him?'

'Those guys weren't shooting fish, mister.'

'But what was that big light?' He was trembling.

'Magnesium flare – Harry fell over a trip wire and set it off, I guess. It means they got the shore wired. I'll have to remember that.' He burrowed deeper into the soil and moved the shotgun to a more comfortable position, preparatory to dozing off. 'Yessir, poor old Harry actually made it. I didn't think he had it in him.'

So they had the shore wired – at that point. They surely didn't have it wired the entire length of the river – counting all the crooks and turns the damned thing must be two thousand miles long or more. The army didn't have *that* much wire. No – only the weak points were booby-trapped. They had wired the immediate area about the bridge either because the structure itself offered concealment to anyone attempting to sneak across *beneath* it, or because they were aware of the underwater cables and knew someone would eventually discover them. Such as poor old Harry – short of wind and not too sound of limb, but he had made it after a long time. *And* a baited trap plus patient prodding.

Why hadn't the army simply cut the cables?

He could think of only one sensible answer to that: they were still being used. Used, say, by those government people still alive and operating the underground fortresses beneath the Pentagon, beneath the rolling Virginia hills. And used, perhaps by the survivors still clinging to Governors Island, the remnants of the First Army. The eastern and western halves of the nation evidently remained in communication. A point to remember.

The night's events somewhat narrowed his future plans. He knew now that all the cables still intact would be heavily guarded, wired and trapped. They would be waiting for him and any other like him at every cable snaking across the river, while Harry's spectacular ending had neither helped nor hindered his own future chances. Harry had been a competent test pilot, not only showing the stream could be crossed, but also that such crossings were expected. As yet, then, he had not broken his promise to the schoolteacher in Florida: *he* had not done any cable-crawling. A sucker had taken care of it for him. Whether or not the promise would be kept in the future remained to be seen. It all depended on whether or not he could find still another way to cross over.

The September night carried a chill. He pulled his coat tighter, turning away from the old man's sobs.

Gary was awake and moving before dawn, not wanting to be caught asleep in an open field when daylight came. He rifled the scavenger's bag for shotgun shells and a box of matches he found there. His two companions still slept, huddled together for warmth. Gary looked down at them for a moment and then swiftly stooped to place his revolver near the old man's hand. In the cold, still darkness he quit the field and left the sleeping men behind.

The air was frosty.

CHAPTER EIGHT

Winter came early, harshly and entirely unexpectedly overnight less than a week afterwards. It came with a bitterly cold wind that swept down from the Canadian plains to engulf the central and north-eastern states, to tumble the mercury by thirty degrees in one night, to lay a thin coating of ice on the quiet lakes and stagnant ponds. Snow began to fall before dawn and continued throughout the day, whipped by swirling gusts of wind, making a farce of the yellow autumn leaves still on the trees. Under the bumpy white blanket the world seemed to grow quiet and still. Nothing seemed to move in the early biting daylight, no man or animal stirring from whatever warmth it possessed. Countless pairs of eyes peered out at the wintry scene in dismayed speculation. The shock of its sudden coming was slow to wear away, and for some sleeping in the open fields it never wore off. They could not move.

Gary slumped in the rear seat of an abandoned car and cursed himself for staying in the North. He should have used his head, should have begun moving south when the first chill hung in the air. He was a fool for staying here.

He could have gone back to the fisherman's cabin in Florida – just to visit, of course. He wouldn't have wintered there. But he could have gone back in response to a sincere invitation: come back and see the kid. Whose kid, he wondered briefly? Or he could have pushed deeper into the South, there were plenty of beaches in Florida; he could have holed up in one of those tourist cabins on the St. Petersburg beach, or gone down to the Keys below Miami. Anywhere to avoid *this*. New Orleans was all right – he could have gone back there. For some reason or other that city wasn't accepting its fate as tragically as the northern river towns. New Orleans attempted to continue as before, its population thinned down, the ferries no longer operating and the Huey Long bridge blocked by a pair of squat tanks. But it went on living after a fashion.

Gary shifted his cramped position on the car seat and told himself again he was a damned fool.

The blast of a shotgun brought him to his knees, his eyes peering through a dirty rear window.

He saw a figure running towards him, towards the old car, a small person who laboured and stumbled as he ran. The figure flung a hasty glance over his shoulder and tried to increase his speed. Gary peered beyond him and discovered the two stalking men. They both carried guns and one of them was reloading as he ran, intent on capturing or killing the fleeing quarry.

Gary snatched up his newly acquired shotgun and flung open the car door, taking care to keep himself out of sight on the rear seat. The little runner continued blindly on towards the car, unaware of his presence or the movement of the door. Gary readied the shotgun. There was a second burst of fire from the pursuers and the youngster screamed, either in pain or terror.

He batted his eyes and waited, trigger finger tensed. It had been a child's scream, a young girl's.

With hoarse, rasping sounds in her dry throat, the girl reached the car and flung herself through the open door to collapse on the floor. Gary reached over and pulled shut the door behind her. The girl whirled and saw him, screamed again and sobbed with a tortured breath. Her eyes were dilated with fright. She looked to be ten or twelve, maybe.

'Cut it out,' he said roughly. 'I'm not going to hurt you.'

She didn't answer him, didn't stop crying and rolling her eyes. With his left hand he reached over and cranked down the rear window, then turned to open the other at his feet. The noise of the two running men came plainly to his ears, their feet making slapping noises in the snow. As best as he could judge, both were following the same path the girl had made, both were running together or nearly so. They should arrive at the car within seconds, approaching on the same side to use the door the child had used.

Gary glanced down. 'Now keep your head down, kid, and

I'll get rid of these guys. You won't get hurt.'

The rear door was yanked open and the girl screamed once more, frantically pushing herself into the far corner.

'I got her! I got the little – '

Gary quietly raised the shotgun to the man's face and fired at his open mouth. The blast cut the head from the shoulders like a hot, ragged knife. Without pause or lost motion, Gary rose swiftly to his knees and poked the smoking barrel through the open door to fire again. It caught the running man in mid-stride, bending him double. As he tumbled to the snow, Gary pumped a second shot into the body. Calmly then, he scanned the horizon for further movement, saw none, and sank back on the seat. With his foot he kicked the severed head outside and shut the door, finally running up the windows.

The child was still in the corner, her face covered by her hands. He wondered how much she had seen. Her crying was hysterical, uncontrolled, and he didn't know how to stop it. She was too little to slap, to gag.

It was more than an hour before he could calm her, could persuade her that he intended no harm, to stop her crying and listen to him, to talk to him. Her story was disconnected and not always intelligent, continually punctuated by fits of dry sobbing. He watched the road and near-by fields, listening to her.

Her name was Sandy, she said. Sandra Hoffman. She was twelve years old and she lived with her two brothers and her parents on the farm 'over there'. Gary could not recall any farmhouse near by and guessed that she had wandered for several miles. Shortly after daylight this morning, she and her older brother Lee – 'he's fifteen, almost' – had gone out rabbit hunting. The early morning hours of the first snowfall is always good rabbit weather, she assured him. Her father had warned them to stay close to the farm but no one suspected any real danger – there had been many 'stealers' about the place, trying to get away with food and clothing, but none offered bodily harm unless caught in the act. She and Lee must have walked further from home than they realised. They hadn't found any rabbits.

Lee had been ahead of her, concentrating on a thicket likely to be concealing rabbits when the two men jumped them. The men had been hiding in the thicket and as they approached, leaped out at them with guns. Lee was carrying his .22 rifle. He fired at them without hesitation, probably in fright rather than fight, and missed. One of the men fired back at him, and Lee fell.

She turned and ran, hiding among the trees for a long time – 'hours and hours' – before she heard them hunting her again. She kept moving around, trying to be quiet, but they finally flushed her. She took to her heels, finding the snow-covered road and running along it until she saw the automobile. They kept shooting at her, too, but they didn't hit her. And now what were they going to do?

Going to do? 'I don't know,' Gary replied absently. 'Let me think about it.'

With her question, a vague idea was born in his mind that he might be able to turn the incident to his advantage. Abandoning the child, simply walking away on her was out of the question; he might have done it if she were older and a boy – if she were her brother Lee, for instance. But he couldn't leave her there in the deserted car. He realised that it could be many tedious weeks, perhaps even bitter months before he could work his way back to the Gulf coast – and there always remained the danger of starving or freezing before reaching it. On the other hand if he stayed in the North, stayed *here*, there was the very real possibility that he could talk his way into a warm and comfortable house for the winter – with food on the table three times a day. He just might be able to use Sandy, *and* the body of her brother, as his entrance into that farmhouse.

It was well worth trying. He sat up.

'The first thing to do,' he said to the girl, 'is to go back and get Lee. Then we'll find your house.'

'But I don't know where he is!' she wailed.

He put out a hand to ruffle the stockingcap pulled down over her hair. 'Aw, that'll be easy for me. All we have to do is follow your backtrail. Say – I'll bet you didn't know I was a scout in the army!'

She gazed at him, round-eyed. 'Was you really?'

'Yep. Used to track Germans all over the place.'

'Japs too?'

He smiled at her and nodded. 'Japs, too. I tracked them all. Let's be moving along now – your dad will be worrying about you.' He opened the door on the opposite side of the car away from the two bodies and helped her out, to lead the way along the erratic, running trail she had left.

The small patch of woods in which she had hidden were not too far distant nor difficult to find. He didn't waste time in trying to follow her wandering footsteps through the woods, but instead began an encircling motion designed to carry him in a complete arc around the trees. A quarter of a mile from where he began, he located the trampled snow where the girl and her two pursuers had entered the woods. Standing there, sighting across the snow, he saw the body as a patch of dark clothing against the white.

'You wait right here,' he told Sandy. 'I'll get Lee.'

She leaned against a cold tree and watched him go.

A part of Lee Hoffman's body had been stripped bare and the flesh cut away. Gary paused for long minutes, staring down at it, gripping his lower lip between his teeth. In an absent sort of way he had speculated on this, had foreseen it if the quarantine lasted long enough and the contaminated survivors grew hungry enough. There had been authenticated reports of it happening among marooned Japanese soldiers during the last war – when the food gave out, the prisoners suffered if there were any, and if not, then one of the soldiers became the unwilling victim. The strongest and the most unprincipled will stay alive in some way, even when that way is winnowed down to cannibalism.

Sooner or later, Gary reflected bitterly, it had to happen east of the Mississippi. Thanks to the damned army and their quarantine, their river patrols. And now here it was.

He stooped low over the body of the boy and wrapped it in clothing, covering it completely so that the girl would see nothing amiss. Hoisting the body over one shoulder and swinging the shotgun in his free hand, he turned and called to Sandy. She came running.

'Is he . . . is he dead?'

'Yes. Let's take him back home now.'

Her lips quivered and he saw that she had been crying while she waited for him. 'I'm lost . . . I don't know where it is.'

'Now stop that stuff! Didn't I tell you I was a scout? A first-class scout?'

'Yes . . . '

'All right then, Sandy, just trust me. Does your farm have any big barns? A tall silo, maybe? Something we could recognise from a distance?'

'Sure, we got them.' She tried to keep her eyes from the burden on his shoulder.

'Then here's what we'll do: see that hill over there, the high one with the two pine trees? Let's climb up there and look for your place – you can shinny up the tree to see better. Okay?'

'Okay.' She fell in behind him, eyes downcast.

Gary completed his plan of action as he walked. When they neared her home, he would send the girl in ahead of him with the news. She was better than a white flag, she and the body across his shoulder, and he would not be shot before he had the opportunity to speak his piece. The farmer, no matter how hostile, would hold off for a few minutes on the strength of the girl and the body of his son. After all – what could be more disarming, more sincere than an utter stranger bringing the two children home? Gary smiled to himself.

'Just stop right there,' Hoffman ordered coldly.

Gary waited without answering. The man stood at the gate to his yard, an old shotgun in his hands. Behind him in the open doorway of the farmhouse Gary glimpsed the farmer's wife, Sandy, and a smaller boy. Fright coupled with alarm was on the woman's face; she didn't look at the newcomer but at the boy's body across his shoulder.

'Put the boy down,' Hoffman said. 'And your gun.'

Gary did as he was told, and backed away a few paces.

Hoffman was a middle-aged man, red of face and weather-beaten from his profession. His eyes were clear and sharp, cautious and distrustful. He approached the body and sank to his knees, keeping the gun on Gary.

'Be careful,' Gary said then. 'Something happened to the boy.'

Hoffman shot him an angry glance. 'What do you mean?'

'I didn't find the boy until it was too late – until the little girl led me back to him. You'll see what I mean when you unwrap him – but be careful! Don't let your wife see it.'

Puzzled but still brimming with anger, the farmer shifted his position to block the view from the doorway and reached out a quivering hand to pull away the coat from the body. He stared at his son's lifeless face and then slowly let his eyes drift along the body.

'God Almighty!' His head jerked up to ask a question but when his lips formed the words no sound came. He knew the answer. Finally – 'Who *did* this?'

'A couple of no-good bastards,' Gary told him without emotion. 'They were after the girl when I caught them.'

Tears had forced in the man's eyes. 'So help me God, when I I get my hands on them . . . !'

'There's nothing you can do to them now, except spit. I said I caught them.'

'You . . . ?'

Gary pointed to his automatic. 'That.'

The farmer stared at him without really seeing him, and then carefully wrapped the clothing about the body and picked it up. 'Bring the guns,' he said to Gary and turned his back. 'Come on up to the house.'

Gary followed him in.

Hoffman carried the body into an inner bedroom, the entire family trailing after. Left alone, Gary looked about the room in which he found himself and sat down, remembering to take off his ragged cap. It seemed to be a combined living room and dining room, opening directly off the kitchen. Something was cooking on the kitchen stove, something that bubbled and hissed, carrying to him a taunting odour that excited his hunger and caused the saliva to flow in his mouth. He held himself in the chair with difficulty, his eyes attempting to see the stove and the kettle around a corner. The room was comfortable and warm and he thought it had been years since he had known anything like it; there was a rocking chair and a long leather couch at the far end, three or four other chairs scattered about and some ancient magazines piled on the floor. From behind a closed door came the sounds of grief.

He pulled his eyes away from the kitchen doorway and tried to shut off the smell of cooking. The wallpaper around him was old and creased with yellow lines, yet it did not detract from the comfort and ease the room suggested. In the centre of the floor stood a heavy oaken table from which the family took their meals, and the faded oilcloth covering it contained hardened, dried spots of spilled food. The little girl's doll lay on the table. Gary looked across the doll and discovered the radio.

He half-rose from his chair, fingers already reaching out to snap the switch, and abruptly sat down again.

Hoffman walked into the room, hand outstretched. Gary stood up, took it.

'I ain't quite got the words to thank you.'

'Not necessary,' Gary told him. 'Any decent man would have done the same.'

'Any man didn't do it,' Hoffman insisted. 'You did.'

'I just happened to be there,' Gary said slowly, almost awkwardly. 'The little girl came running to me . . . ' He released the farmer's hand, sat down when the other did. There was a moment of strained silence. 'If it's all the same to you, I'll move along. There's nothing more I can do to help you, I guess.'

'Leave?' Hoffman eyed him with astonishment. 'By God, you'll not leave! I can't let you up and walk out of here after what you've done for me, man. I owe you a debt I can't ever repay!'

'You don't owe me anything,' Gary contradicted him. His eyes drifted towards the kitchen. 'I wouldn't take pay.'

The farmer was staring at him. 'You're hungry!' he said with sudden surprise. 'The devil, I should have thought of that.' He jumped out of his chair and took Gary's arm, pulling him towards the kitchen. 'Come on out here – you can eat until it runs out of your ears!' He snatched the lid from the hot kettle and burned his fingers, swearing absently. 'The Lord knows we ain't got much left in this crazy world, but we *have* got food. You can have all you want of it.'

Gary accompanied Hoffman late that afternoon when the farmer took his son's body to a snow-covered hill for burial. He offered to help but was politely turned down, and told the farmer he would go along anyway to keep watch – one of them should keep their eyes open that far from the house.

He said nothing more while the silent man dug the grave, knowing that his remark would take root. When the grave was completed and the body ready for burial, the remainder of the family joined the two of them on the hillside, and Hoffman opened an old family Bible. Gary stood a short distance away, his cap off, listening to the halting words and the weeping of the bereaved mother. He slowly and silently paced the hill, continually watching the fields around them and seeing to it that his watch crossed and recrossed the vision of the farmer. That too would take root.

He felt no remorse over the boy's death for the boy had meant nothing to him; his stomach was full – overly full – for the first time since he had left the fisherman's cabin on the Florida beach; and he knew a vast satisfaction and a return of his old cockiness. Completely without cynicism or qualms of conscience he was putting on an act, an act designed to win him a warm winter home. He counted on the farmer's noticing it and bringing up the matter first.

The brief service over, they returned to the house.

By the next morning he had it.

Hoffman brought it up over the breakfast table. 'Sandy tells me you're a soldier? In the army?'

'I was – yes. I was attached to the Fifth Army in Chicago, before the bombing. But they wouldn't let me come across the river to rejoin them.' He reached for another helping.

'Them devils don't let nobody across. I know a couple of fellas who tried it.' He paused. 'You a good shot?'

'Yes,' Gary answered frankly. 'Sharpshooter. Why?'

'I want to offer you a job – I ain't forgetting what we owe you.'

Gary grinned across the table at him. 'Mr. Hoffman, I told you, you don't owe me a thing. And as for the job – I've never worked on a farm in my life. I can't milk a cow.'

'Wouldn't expect you to – we can take care of that. It'll be hard doing without Lee next summer, but we can take care of that. You would take care of the soldiering.'

'What?' He stopped eating.

'Be our lookout, our guard. What do they call them in the army? Sentry. We've had one blamed thief after another around here, day in and day out. They've been robbing us blind, and I can't run the place and keep chasing them too. That would be your job – keeping thieves off the place.'

'Well . . . I don't know what to say. I sort of figured on going down south for the winter . . . '

'I can't pay you nothing,' Hoffman continued. 'Not in money. We ain't got none left and you couldn't spend it anyway. But we can offer you a good home and the best eating in this part of the country; my wife's a fine cook!'

Gary glanced at the woman and then the two children. 'I'd certainly like to, Mr. Hoffman, but – '

'Please?' Sandy broke in.

He glanced down the table to find the girl shyly smiling at him, a pleading invitation in her eyes.

'Do you really want me to stay, Sandy?'

She nodded eagerly. 'Pretty please?'

'Well . . . ' He scratched his ragged beard, petending to consider it. Finally his gaze swung back to Hoffman. 'Oh well, all right.' And then he added quickly, 'Until spring, anyway.'

'Fine! Believe me, we're glad to hear of it – all of us. Now eat up. You've got to put on some weight.'

'Can I borrow a razor?' Gary asked. 'And if you have a pair of scissors handy I'd like to trim off this hair. I haven't been to a barbershop in a long time.'

Staring at his newly-pale image in the yellowed mirror later that morning, he winked at the lathered man in the glass. 'Very neat, Corporal Gary.' The image agreed.

Gary studied the terrain about the farm buildings, conscious of the one blind approach to their defences. Beyond the barn the ground fell away sharply, a rough pasture land that dipped down to a frozen creek nearly three-quarters of a mile away. Anyone approaching from that direction need only keep the barn between himself and the house, to be able to come very near without detection. Gary found baling wire in a machine shed and strung trippers across the slope beyond the barn, fastening a rusty cowbell to the outermost wire. The next snow would hide everything from sight.

He set up a pattern of watching at night and sleeping during the day, knowing from experience that the most dangerous marauders would approach only under cover of darkness. In his nightly prowling he looked for and expected every trick of the trade that he himself had practised, knowing there were men out there as smart as he, and as hungry as he had been. Awake at night and sleeping during the day, but still unwilling to miss the day's hot meals, he had himself awakened for each of them. And after dusk he stalked about the deserted land, prying around the buildings, alert for sight or sound of any moving thing. The farmer's family slept soundly, trusting him.

Gary came into the house one evening just at bedtime, just as Sandy was snapping off the radio. The illumination was slowly dying behind the transparent dial and he watched it fade with startled eyes.

'That thing *works*!'

'What?' Hoffman turned around. 'Oh – sure it does. Didn't you know it?' The farmer shrugged. 'Ain't worth a dang, though. All the time them silly comics is blabbering, and it's always selling something we can't buy.'

'But how?' Gary demanded impatiently, indicating the single, flickering kerosene lamp the farmer held in his hand. 'Where do you get the electricity for a radio over here?'

'The windmill – Lee fixed it up for us last winter.'

'What about the windmill?'

'The boy fixed it, he was a mighty smart kid – knew his way around with electricity and machinery. He hooked a generator up to the windmill somehow. I don't know how he did it – if it ever goes out of whack, that'll be the end of it. Lee was a good kid. It plays all right as long as the wind holds out. Kinda fades away, sometimes.'

'A radio!' Gary was fascinated with it. 'Well I'll be damned – a radio right here in the house with me and I never knew it worked.' He went over to it, caressed the cabinet with his fingers and let his nails flick the glass of the dial. 'I want to play it.'

'Help yourself,' Hoffman returned. 'Kinda keep it down though, will you? The wife's a light sleeper.'

'What? Oh, sure, sure.' The cabinet felt hot under his hand. 'Sure.'

Hoffman turned away. 'Good night.'

Gary was too entranced with the set to answer. The farmer left, carrying with him the only kerosene lamp and the room was plunged into darkness. Sandy's voice was audible for a few seconds and then the bedroom door slammed, cutting off her words and the last stray gleam of the light.

Impatiently, Gary flung back the blackout curtains at the windows, letting in the faint light of the clouded moon and reflected snow. He never used a light. The night outside was cold and quiet. He ran back to the radio, sank to his knees before it and excitedly twisted the knob which furnished electric current. The small dial gained life, bringing the imprinted numbers into sharp relief and bringing a hum to the speaker. His burning eagerness to *hear* stopped his fingers, made him aware of the peculiar thrill the glow and sound had given him. A year, a year and a half ago, this was nothing, but now it was everything. This was next to life itself. This was people somewhere on the other side of the river, healthy people, safe people, talking to each other and continuing their lives. This was civilisation, and sanity, and warmth, and food, this was one man on friendly terms with the next. This was what he had lost a long time ago and despaired of ever having again.

Quickly he snapped the radio off and counted the long seconds, then eagerly turned it on again only to see the light come up, to listen to the growing power of the set. There was a strange tightness in his stomach as he touched a second control knob and moved it a fraction of an inch.

A girl was singing.

He found her in the middle of a word, on a syllable that at once brought the entire word into his mind as though he had heard it from the beginning, and that word and the next few cast the image of the entire sentence on his consciousness so that he could not remember where he had come in, could readily imagine that he had heard it all. She was singing a slow song, a sweet and sad song about leaves of brown that tumbled down and somewhere behind her where it shouldn't have been interfering a bell tinkled faintly.

He frowned at that, annoyed with the bell and knowing it shouldn't be there.

A bell. He leaped to his feet and dashed for the door, snatching up the automatic shotgun as he sped through it.

In his haste he forgot the radio, forgot to shut the door after him as he ran across the yard and slammed through the wire gate of the old fence. Running silently, lightly, he was careful to keep the hulking barn between him and the sloping pasture land beyond it. Once in the moon-shadow of the structure he slowed, trotted cautiously alongside the building and came to a full stop just short of the corner. He listened. There was no sound.

Gary flattened himself against the wall and inched his head past the corner. Down the slope a dark bundle of nothing lay on the ground. As he watched, a slow movement of an arm and hand seemed to detach itself from the shapeless mass, seemed to reach out probing fingers for the wires he had strung there. The dark figure was well past the outer wire which had held the bell.

And behind him, although he could not hear it, he knew the radio was playing softly and a girl was singing to him. All for him. The sound of his shooting would stop her, would end the quiet contentment of the voice and the moment, as the family roused from their beds and rushed into the room. He didn't want the family there, didn't want the interference, didn't want to answer their foolish questions and waste time getting them back into bed again. The girl would be gone.

There was no sound but the windmill pumping in the clouded night. Below him, the figure had passed another wire.

Gary backed away from the corner, retreated alongside the barn until he came to a small door. Unlatching it, he went inside and made his way through the gloom to a corner where cast-off machinery was kept. Feeling around on the floor, his fingers touched an iron rod and he picked it up, hefted it, judging its weight and striking power. It would serve. He let himself out and quietly latched the door behind him, careful to avoid a betraying noise. Once more he took up his post at the corner of the barn, concealed in the shadows and impatient with the stranger for taking so much time to climb the slope.

Damn him, damn him, why didn't he hurry?

Immediately afterwards, Gary thought to dispose of the body. To leave the man here for discovery on the morrow would only raise a furore, cause questions, perhaps more of that confounded weeping. The corpse had nothing in his pockets.

He circled the barn very slowly, peering with feverish eyes across the fields and pasturage, but if the fellow had a companion there was no sight of him. Nothing else moved under the clouded moon. Finally satisfied, he at last returned to where the body lay and stooped to hoist it across his shoulders. Swinging the shotgun in his free hand, he set off in a fast walk down the slope towards the distant creek. The man was heavy and his shoulder tired; twice he had to dump the body into the snow and stop for a short rest. It seemed to Gary that an hour had passed before he reached the frozen creek and threw the body down on to the ice.

The woman and the two kids would not come this far from the house, not any more, and it would be spring before Hoffman had occasion to come this way.

Gary turned and ran for the farmhouse.

Just inside the yard gate he hurled himself to the frozen ground and aimed at the yawning door, seeking movement within. The man's voice was low, soothing. It went on and on without variation. Gary frowned, jumped forward and halted again, listening to the voice. The voice stopped and some instrument struck three tiny notes.

The notes stirred his memory and he climbed to his feet, swearing softly at himself. The radio was still on. Gary let himself through the door and closed it behind him, eyes darting about the room. There was nothing, no one other than himself. A second male voice came from the speaker.

The girl was gone.

CHAPTER NINE

Gary ran to the radio and crouched down before it.

'. . . while in the west the icy grip of winter caused another tragic accident, this one near Laramie, Wyoming. A heavily loaded troop train running behind schedule was struck from the rear by a speeding freight, and the last four cars demolished. The engineer of the freight, himself hurt, blamed lack of visibility; it was snowing heavily, he said, and he had extreme difficulty seeing the track signals, much less the lights on the rear of the troop train. Police on the scene have not released the casualty figures, and military authorities said the train was en route to the Mississippi frontier, carrying replacements.

'And that brings us to the next piece of news, happy news for some men in the line and their women waiting at home. Rotation goes on, winter or not, and many weary soldiers can look forward to Christmas at home. An army spokesman said fresh troops are arriving weekly at the Mississippi and Canadian frontiers, releasing those with the longest months of service. Authorities have consistently refused to divulge the number of troops now guarding those frontiers – but, the spokesman reminded me again today, there are more than enough to protect the nation from the few enemy agents known to be roaming around that desolate land. Those agents are welcome to the contaminated states, the hard-eyed soldiers tell me, welcome to the dead and vacant nothing that is east of the river. *And* when we get ready to take it again, what few remain will run like frightened rabbits.'

Gary sat down hard, staring at the lighted dial.

'Only a few months ago, you will remember, the army security office released the details of one such agent who attempted to cross the river *under* it, at an undisclosed point along the Minnesota shore. He was cut down amid a hail of bullets before he could climb from the water, and the river swallowed his body. A pity, I think, for once we capture one of these fellows we can definitely prove his origin and his nationality to the world.

'Meanwhile, weak signals continue to trickle in from the Pentagon, proving that some brave Americans are still alive in that underground fortress – quite possibly the only Americans still living east of the Mississippi. A few days ago I was privileged to see some rare photographs obtained by reconnaissance planes flying over parts of Illinois and Kentucky – photographs which showed no living thing in those unfortunate states. No smoke curled upwards from chimneys, no children or adults moved about the houses and yards, there was not even a dog to track the smooth expanse of snow. Without a doubt, the only American survivors are those who have secreted themselves in an underground bastion, while the despicable enemy agents patrol the rest.'

'You're a lying sonofabitch and you know it!' Gary hurled back at the smooth voice.

'And now, closer to home . . . Right here in federal court today a former Missouri farmer named Edward Evans won his long-contested case against the government. Evans, who with thousands of others was hastily evacuated from the frontier when the bombs fell, protested that the government did not allow him anything near a fair price for his land. The Evans farm lay entirely within the ten mile strip now called "No Man's Land", and of course he lost it all, not even being allowed to harvest his crops. A federal jury agreed with the distressed farmer, awarding him twenty dollars an acre more than the government offered. Other such suits are expected to follow.

'Street cars are running again, after a long absence from our streets, and I must say they make a strange, if welcome, sight. Following the ban on pleasure travel due to the critical shortage of oil and gasoline, public buses were next to feel the pinch and their schedules were drastically curtailed. This in turn played havoc with the habits of bus riders and local defence plants reported a serious increase in absenteeism and tardiness. Street cars were the answer, and happily the rails had never been ripped up. Let's welcome back the noisy old trolley and save gasoline.

'And as for rubber tyres! Mister, mention that word around town and you are knee-deep in argument. Akron, Ohio – if that unfortunate city still stands – will have number one priority when we march across the river once more.

'An optimistic note in today's news comes from the postal department. By next summer, declares the postmaster general, the cost of mailing a first class letter should be down to about ten cents – perhaps even less if other ways can be found to bolster post-office revenue. There is also reason to believe that smaller cities and towns – as well as rural routes – may again be receiving mail every day instead of every second or third day as they do now. You may expect this before next summer. The loss of books, magazines, advertising and other types of third and fourth class mail plunged the department into the red, of course, and it had been a slow uphill fight coming back. I'm sure that my listeners will be pleased with the prospect of loosening that wartime belt by at least one notch.'

'Oh, go to hell!' Gary reached out angrily and shut off the radio.

The suave voice was lying with every other sweet sentence it uttered, lying or spreading propaganda of the most transparent sort. He had seen the army working *that* line of endeavour too well in Italy to be taken in by it, had seen the effects of smooth talk on newly conquered, vastly bewildered Germans. It seemed all right at the time, seemed the thing to do to a defeated enemy. They had to be re-educated, given refresher courses in democracy, and what better way to do it than feed them propaganda pills sugar-coated with news? And now the United States was receiving the same treatment from the same hands – the twenty-two United States west of the all-important river. Those twenty-two states were under martial law, no question of it. The radio announcer had unconsciously confirmed it by his honeyed words, his phrasing of the news; in a situation such as the present one the army passed on what was broadcast, what was printed.

He was still alive, still walking around in the contaminated zone, therefore declared the army he was an enemy agent. What could be the reason for spreading that? To cover up their inability to accept him back, to hide their fear of him and others like him? Or was it the foundation for something else to come, the preparatory steps of reconstruction such as the schoolteacher had hinted? Was he branded an enemy agent for the sake of convenience – when the mopping-up process came?

In the year and a half since awakening in that dirty hotel room he had not met one person who might be such an agent, who might actually have entered the country for war-making purposes. He had seen only countless hundreds of ordinary people fighting to stay alive – to prolong their lives until the day the government came to their rescue. Of course the chimneys didn't smoke, not any more, not during the daylight hours unless you wanted strangers. He had cautioned Hoffman's wife of that folly and she now did her cooking under cover of darkness. And of course there were no more dog tracks on the snow – dogs had vanished long before cannibalism came into the picture. But there *were* people in and about many of the houses; it might be that they no longer rushed out to stare at an aeroplane overhead, but they were there even though the photographer chose to ignore them. There were thousands of them still alive in the contaminated zone – waiting for what? Waiting to be 'reconstructed'? Was that the real reason in telling the western states they no longer existed.

Rotation of troops – that was a sweet one! Troops were rotated by the trainload only when several thousand of them were in the line, and why should several thousand be needed when only a handful of 'enemy agents' ran free across the river? Did good tax-paying citizens with tight belts swallow that? Had they all lost the ability to think for themselves?

That dumb lout Harry had been an enemy agent, so they quickly knocked him off. Harry would have lacked the humour to appreciate the joke. Harry would have demanded a better reward for the effort of crawling the cable. But crawl it he did, neglecting to give the password, and they cut him down before he could leave the water. Then maybe a high-flying fish fell over that tripwire and set off the flare, while afterwards someone in a radiation suit came down to the shore and kicked the fish back into the water. But of course the army could get away with that sort of thing – the ten-mile strip of No Man's Land took care of leaks. There were no civilians anywhere within ten miles of the river line.

There had been but one thing in the news broadcast that caught his imagination and held it – those brave, unknown warriors who still held the Pentagon cellars.

That was worth looking into – next spring when he could travel again.

He had guessed that the intact cables under the bridge meant that east-west communications remained open, and this was proof of it. The incoming signals may or may not be weak – you couldn't take that lying announcer's word for it – but signals were received. In view of the implied declaration of war on survivors such as himself, there would be little point in mentioning still other survivors in Washington – eventually they would have to be accounted for as other than 'enemy agents'. Top brass, therefore, had some reason for their still being 'alive', some reason for talking about them. Gary decided that the cellar holdouts definitely needed investigation. Next spring.

He reached up listlessly and turned the radio on again. There was no mounting thrill this time as the dial glowed, nothing but an undefined dullness within him, no impatience in waiting for the instrument to speak.

It spoke with a slick new voice.

'Yes, I said Mother Mahaffey's Candies are back! Good news indeed for lovers of sweet things – government restrictions on sugar have been lifted and once more you may help yourself to the delicious candies from Mother Mahaffey's kitchens! Just listen to the goodies she has for you: crisp and crunchy pecan twists . . . creamy caramels . . . toothsome bittersweet creams . . . the utter goodness of home-made chocolates! Don't delay, get some today, treat that best girl to a treasure she'll long remember! Mother Mahaffey's Candies, the best in the West. There is a Mother Mahaffey Candy Kitchen near you.

'You have been listening to the late news round-up by Judson May, your Mother Mahaffey Candy Man. The following is transcribed – '

Gary savagely twisted away the transcription, telling the announcer in short, angry words his opinion of him, Judson May *and* Mother Mahaffey. Mother Mahaffey at least would experience difficulty in following his advice, were she a mind to try. The dial pointer came to rest on still another unctuous male voice and he twisted it again, to discover the sound of music beneath his fingers. He didn't recognise the song, had not the slightest idea what it was all about, but the music pleased him. He stretched out full length on the floor and listened to it.

It hurt him.

For hours the music had caused him pain, bringing out his abject loneliness and underscoring the world he had lost. He stood at a window watching the empty fields. A heavily clouded sky had long since obscured the moon, bringing the threat of a new snow. Periodically during the night he had torn himself away from the radio to swing hastily about the farm buildings, scanning the vast reaches for visitors.

And as the hour grew late, one by one the stations left the air, the announcer invariably bidding him a pleasant good night. One by one he chased the departing stations over the dial, avidly seeking a new one to replace the old. Each time he felt the brief fear that there would be no more stations waiting for him, and each time he tuned in another. The number of them steadily narrowed until finally there was but one and he clung to it possessively, hoping against hope it would stay with him all night. During the long hours he had even come to accept the intervening announcements and advertisements, to wait out nervously the long-winded appeals for the purchase of lotions and medicines and shrubs, of war bond drives and pleas for scrap iron, of short and worthless news bulletins and idle horseplay on the part of the speaker. Eventually the music came back.

Some of the numbers he knew and remembered of years before, some he had sung or tried to sing in saloons and Red Cross loafing rooms, a very few went all the way back to the bitter days in Italy and France. Others were undoubtedly as old but he hadn't heard them before – that, or had not paid enough attention to recognise them now. And once in a while there was something he was positive was new, brand-new. The recordings having men singers annoyed him but still he listened, for a year and a half is too long a time. Those sung by women hurt the most – the women and their words reminded him how desperately lonely he was.

He talked aloud to himself, and didn't care. He had done that in Europe a decade before and the mark of loneliness clung to him ever afterward. Not that he cared. He had not bothered to break the habit when he moved into the farmhouse, although he often found the children staring at him. They'd learn when they grew up – if they grew up. So he talked back to some of the women who sang to him – it depended on what they sang, how they said it; and sometimes he threw a bitter word at the announcer, disgusted with his asininity.

The world was gone. He knew it now with finality.

He was alone in it, just himself, and those other minor figures who moved about did so only as foils, as shadows from which he must protect himself or die, or other shadows on whom he must prey or die. There was no one else alive with a life he could feel, no living thing he could trust, eat with, sleep with. She was back there . . .

He snapped his finger, started at the sound.

Irma. That had been her name – Irma something. The nineteen-year-old kid who had been with her college class on an exploration trip when the bombs fell. Irma who had come back home to loot jewellery shops when he found her, found her by the shattering noise of a plate glass window. It was difficult now to recall what she was like – young yes, but not little or undeveloped. She had looked like a sixteen-year-old but still there had been something of a woman about her. He could remember the brilliant blue of her eyes the first time he saw them – that night when he pinned her to the street, holding the light on her face. Her hair? He had the vague impression it had been brown. She had thrown herself at him the next morning in the hotel, the morning she had thought him gone, and her tears had wet his naked chest. That was Irma.

They had eaten together while sitting on the kerbing before some abandoned grocery store, or sitting on a hotel bed, or behind the wheel of a car. Eaten and lived together for many days back before he realised the world was lost. She had gone with him while he collected his weapons, his first car, his initial stock of supplies for the hungry days he supposed were ahead until he could get back to the army. Days! Irma had kept him close company, only to part at the bridge.

That had been a damned fool thing to do. They should have stayed together. Irma had been a pretty girl, would be pretty still – if she were living. She'd be twenty-one now, according to her figures. Attractive figure.

And after Irma?

The string bean who had walked up to them in the Tennessee hills. Sally. No other name, just Sally, who could be nice to them both but preferred Oliver, the schoolteacher. He wondered briefly if *he* had a son, or had Oliver? Sally was pretty much of a nonentity in his memory, just a woman who had been there at the time and left no indelible mark on him. Somewhat similar to the woman in New Orleans for a couple of weeks after leaving Sally. *Her* name was already lost, and the memory of her nearly so until he concentrated on it.

Three. In a year and a half. And *that* for a man who liked to boast around the barracks of his numberless conquests.

The world was gone. He stared through the window at the vast emptiness of it, wondering if it would ever again come alive. Just behind him an unseen woman sang softly. She sang from another world across the void because this one was gone, populated only by the quick and the dead; she sang from a world which used to exist for everybody but was now permanently restricted. She mouthed the words and carried the melody as though nothing untoward had happened, as though her singing – and the commercial appeal to follow – were all that mattered.

That hurt, too.

The casual acceptance of the propaganda and the news reports that they alone still lived, while all else was death. The willingness to believe that only they were safe and healthy while east of the river nothing but sure death and enemy agents stalked the land. How much will people believe without questioning? Did none of them stop to consider that *someone* might still be alive over there . . . that *someone* was listening to their broadcasts and knowing how false they were? Hadn't it ever occurred to any of them that their programmes were being picked up by people who used to be in their world, people who could be hurt as they listened?

What if he had a telephone? Supposing that by some strange means he had a phone and he could casually pick up the receiver and put through a call to the radio station. To ask for a song, say. People did that all the time.

'What?' the surprised announcer would ask.

'I said,' Gary would have to repeat, 'that I'm calling from something-or-other Wisconsin, and I want you to play a number.'

'But you can't be!' that disbelieving man would answer him. 'There's no life in Wisconsin.'

'There is, and don't believe everything you hear. How about playing *Clementine* for me? Or maybe, *Cruising Down the River*? That's a good one these days.'

'I can't, do you hear? I refuse. You're dead, Judson May said you were dead.'

'Upstick Judson May! You going to play me a song or not?'

'This is a trick! There's no one alive on the other side of the river. You're attempting to hoax me!' And he would hang up in anger. Or sudden fear.

And when the security office heard *that* they would immediately get the station on the line, or perhaps send around an officious major. It had been a despicable occurrence and they would caution the announcer to say no more about it. Might upset the citizens. There are some things they could not be trusted to know. Under cover of darkness a wily enemy agent had surreptitiously crossed the river and made his way to a telephone. It was to be regretted of course and it would not happen again. Alert sentries had cut the man down before he could climb out of the water. All quiet. All safe and snug west of the line of quarantine.

He stood with his chilled back against the barn, looking down across the sloping pasture towards the distant creek. The ancient pipe given him by the farmer was unlit but he continued to hold it in his mouth, savouring the stale taste of it.

The approaching dawn was bitterly cold and sulking behind the heavy cloud blanket, revealing itself only as a faint brightening close to the eastern horizon, a gradual increase in the visibility over the frozen fields. He saw the telltale marks of the night just past, the slow and crawling path the stranger had made coming up the slope, the infinite twists and turns to avoid the trip wire. The trail led up to the side of the barn, up to the corner where he had waited for the man. Before he had covered it with a shuffling foot there had been a frozen splotch of blood, black in the faint light of the new day. He saw his deeply indented footsteps where he had carried the heavy body back down the slope to the frozen creek, and returning, the light and wide-spaced marks he had left on the run.

But the first girl had been gone, the girl he wanted.

A short while ago that last station had left the air, left him scrabbling frantically over an empty dial searching for another voice, another bar of music. There were no more. The loneliness descended twofold then, and the hurt deepened. The airwaves were as empty as the land around him. He shut off the radio and was depressed by the silence of the room, by the emptiness of it after his new-found companions had left. Pulling on the borrowed overcoat he wore and taking up his gun, he had quit the house to make another patrol of the buildings, striding in a great circle through the nearer fields alert for fresh footprints leading towards the house. Eventually he had come upon the slurred trail made by last night's visitor, and followed it up to the barn.

He stood there, cold and forlorn.

Some day – out there, across those snowy wastes – would come the conquering army from across the Mississippi, mopping up the stragglers and paving the way for the reconstruction of a half-wrecked nation. Hoffman and his wife, the younger boy and Sandy – all stragglers, blocking their path. The four of them, four 'enemy agents' rushing out to greet returning troops with heartfelt cries of welcome. What a shock they would receive.

Oliver's speculative medical aid was pretty much of a lost dream . . . what was it he had said? 'It all depends on the prevailing mood of high brass *and* the state of medicine on the day bridges are reopened. If the stragglers can be cleansed and cured by some revolutionary medical means – well then, welcome back to the United States!' And 'The patrols would gather up residue and test it for contamination; when the tested matter no longer revealed a danger, the crisis would be over except for mopping up the stragglers.'

A lost dream with a brutal awakening for many people; people like the Hoffmans who clung to their farm and what few possessions that remained to them, awaiting the day of deliverance. He didn't want to be here when that day came. He didn't want want to see the terrified expression on Sandy's face again. And now he was convinced that day was coming, that *kind* of day . . . Judson May glibly spouting his lines had all but said it. Judson May was parroting the words and schemes placed in his mouth by high brass. High brass *and* the lamentable state of medicine had left no room in their blueprints of reconstruction for surviving stragglers, and a good many 'enemy agents' would be eliminated before Akron, Ohio, could be rebuilt again.

He wanted to be a thousand miles from Sandy when that day arrived. Sandy wouldn't be nineteen for seven more years.

With a start he came to, saw that snow was falling. The eastern glow was gone, diffused by the clouds, but day had arrived over the fields. He stepped to the corner of the barn and looked back towards the house, looked up at the patched chimney where a thin curl of smoke drifted upwards. Hoffman's wife was cooking breakfast before damping the fires for the day. She needn't worry now, not with the snow. A fairly heavy snow would conceal the smoke a reasonable distance away.

He was hungry and turned his steps towards the house, casting one last glance behind him to see if the marauder's trail was disappearing. Sandy poked about the barn occasionally and he didn't want her to see that.

Come spring, he promised himself aloud, the *first* sign of spring, and he was going to have a look at the heroes hiding in the Washington cellar. To hell with this weather.

CHAPTER TEN

Blue-sky summer. Warm, mellow, peaceful and relaxing, summer in Ohio. He supposed he was in Ohio – someone had chopped down the highway markers and probably used them for firewood the previous winter. He made it a habit to avoid the cities. It didn't matter; if he wanted to think he was in Ohio, then he was there. He lay flat on his back in the tall, uncut grass watching the shapeless clouds drift along. A wandering ant explored the skin of his hand but he was too content to brush it away. The sky, the rolling clouds and the smell of the grass.

He had really intended to be here sooner, had wanted to be nearer Washington by this time. Taking leave of Sandy and her parents had been a difficult thing; they had kept him long past his decided departure date, long past the day his eyes began searching the far horizon in eager yearning. He had finally got away from them only by promising that he would return in the early autumn.

Gary watched the slothful clouds in the blue and doubted very much that he would keep that promise.

He *would* like to go back in perhaps eight or ten years – if he were able – to see Sandy. That would be worth going back to; but to return sooner than that, as early as next winter, no. Next winter he intended to exercise common sense and head back to the Gulf coast, perhaps back to that fisherman's shack on the water where an invitation awaited him. And after that, as deep into Florida as he could go. There he would not freeze unless the weather tricked him, would not starve as long as fish swam in the sea.

Ohio was fine in the warm, lazy summer . . . so fine and comfortable that he felt no alarm when the distant sound of shooting broke out. He lay still, listening to it, knowing that a sizable party was involved by the number of guns and knowing too that it was too far away to involve him.

An answering machine-gun brought him to his feet.

Machine-guns! Machine-guns meant soldiers, unless somewhere a band of marauders had come into possession of such a weapon. Barring that, soldiers meant...

He was running lightly and swiftly towards the firing. Soldiers this far from the Mississippi could mean the mopping-up process had begun, that the river had been crossed and high brass was clearing the land of enemy agents and contaminated survivors. Gary leaped a sagging barbed wire fence and sped across the field. As he ran he found himself praying – praying not to any Creator he may have believed in but praying in his own expressive, violent tongue that it was not so, that the western states had not come to reclaim the bombed land. The land was harsh, hungry and terrible but he suddenly didn't want to lose it, to give it up in exchange for what *they* offered. He had hated it but now he didn't want to lose it; had often cursed it and the obscene fate which had placed him there but now it was preferable. The remainder of his lean, starved life there was better than the firing squads. Hell, he was only thirty . . . Thirty-something. He didn't want to die now!

Gary flung himself down behind a knoll and inched his way towards the grassy top. The firing was loud in his ears. He paused just short of the crest, ready to leap and run in retreat, and then hitched his shotgun forward to part the grasses shutting off the view. He stiffened.

A battered, paved highway wound along the valley floor less than half a mile distant and nothing but two small trucks occupied that highway. Two trucks! With mounting excitement he wriggled forwards to gain a better view. Two green-panelled army trucks somewhat resembling that armoured mail truck he had used years before; two trucks, halted and under siege in the lonely road. He looked to see why they had stopped. One truck was partially nosed over into the roadside ditch, and from this distance it looked as if a tyre had been shot away, leaving it helpless. The second had stopped a few yards ahead. Gary studied the tableau. Rifle fire was pouring from the cabs of both vehicles, snapping the tall grass along the nearer ditch and searching out the terrain behind it.

After a moment he located the machine-gun. It was barking from a small broken window in the rear of the disabled truck. He saw a body lying on the road.

Army trucks, their blunt noses pointed westward towards the distant Mississippi.

Instantly he concocted a plan of action. Half rising, he sped several yards downhill towards the raging battle and dropped again into the concealing grass – waited long seconds before rising and running again, following a zigzag path down the slope. As he worked his way in hasty, cautious spurts towards the stalled trucks he knew he was visible from the road, knew they couldn't help but see him, yet no bullet spat his way. As he drew nearer he ran shorter distances before dropping to earth again, putting up his head for quick reconnaissance before making another dash. His method of approach should be obvious to the men in the trucks, should be familiar to them.

Finally he located five men on the ground before him, fairly well hidden from the roadway but in positions that were open to his view. Four of the five men firing at the road; the fifth lay still.

When he was within easy range he fell flat on the ground and opened on them a murderous fire.

Startled, they turned to stare at him, half-rising in their sudden fear. He fired again and one man fell. Rifle fire from their now unprotected rear increased sharply and the surviving three jerked around, aware of the trap. Abruptly the three broke cover and ran, attempting to flee along the ditch. Gary rose to his knees and loosed a final blast before sinking to the ground. The machine-gun opened up once more as the three ran into its range, and then it was quiet.

Gary could almost feel the solid silence.

Without moving, he shouted, 'Hold your fire!'

Someone in the truck answered him. 'Come out with your hands up.'

Very slowly he rose to his feet, hands high, still clutching the shotgun in a doubled fist. He cautiously made his way across the ditch to stand at the edge of the roadway, peering at the two men in the nearer cab.

'Put down the gun.'

Gary hesitated. 'Not until you cover me – I don't want to get shot in the back.'

'You're covered. Put it down fast!'

He stooped to lay it on the cement.

'All right now, who are you?'

'Corporal Russell Gary . . . used to be with the Fifth in Chicago.'

A helmeted head appeared in the window of the cab. The helmet bore a stripe of white paint. Gary absently added, 'Sir.'

'Do you carry identification, Corporal?' the officer asked suspiciously.

'Yes, sir.' He dug down under his clothing to bring up the two dog-tags hanging on a chain.

The lieutenant peered at them and then up at the man. 'Well, I don't mind saying thanks! You certainly helped us out of a hole.' He paused. 'Are you alone?'

'Yes, sir.' Gary looked down the road at the sprawled bodies. 'Except for the casualties, sir.'

There was a moment of silence as the officer sought for words. Gary stared at him, at the second face looking over his shoulder.

The second face suggested, 'Ask him about Chicago, Lieutenant.'

'A-bombed,' Gary said without waiting for the other to repeat the questions. 'Hundreds of A-bombs. The place is just a pile of ashes now.'

'How did you escape?' was the quick retort.

'I wasn't there, sir. I was on recruiting duty downstate.' He thought to volunteer more. 'The whole damned country is washed out, sir. A-bombs and disease everywhere. There can't be more than a couple of thousand people left.'

'That many? Are you certain?'

'Yes, sir. I've covered all the ground between Chicago and Florida in the last couple of years, sir. There was a lot more that first year, but I'd say there's only a few thousand this summer, Lieutenant.'

'Well, I'll be damned. They said –'

'Yes, sir?'

'Good work, Corporal, good work. We can't thank you enough. Now we'll have to repair that tyre and move on.'

'Sir?'

'Yes?'

'I was sort of hoping you could take me with you.'

'Out of the question,' the lieutenant snapped. 'You are contaminated. Was that why you opened fire on the enemy? I commend you, Corporal, but I can do no more.'

Gary stared at him, his bearded face a carefully framed picture of disappointment. 'I can't . . . ? But sir, I . . . '

'No!'

Gary shuffled his feet, made as if to leave and then turned back once more. 'Say, Lieutenant, got anything to eat?'

'None to spare, Corporal; I'm sorry. Our supplies must last out the trip. And now move down the road, please. We have to replace that tyre.'

Eagerly he said, 'I'll fix it for you, sir. If you can let me have something to eat.' He waited for a moment and then added, 'Please, Lieutenant – food is damned scarce.'

The officer examined him, his thin body and ragged clothing. He turned once to exchange glances with the other man in the car and then faced Gary again. He struggled to keep his face emotionless.

'All right, Corporal. We haven't too much ourselves but I dare say you need it worse than we do. Now – the tyre.'

'Yes, sir,' he started forward. 'Give me the jack.'

'Stop right there! Don't approach the truck, man, you're contaminated. We haven't our suits on. We'll throw the jack out to you.'

'Suits?' Gary repeated stupidly.

'Radiation suits – have to wear them in this damned place. Now about that tyre . . . '

'Yes, sir!' Gary walked around to the front of the truck and squinted at the wrecked rubber. That tyre would never roll again. 'Keep a sharp look-out, Lieutenant. Don't want somebody to take a shot at me.' He slid the jack under the front axle and began pumping. The wheel slowly rose in the air.

Gary was in high humour but he was careful not to let it show in his face. *These,* he told himself with bitter amusement, these were some of the surviving heroes from the eastern cellars. The very adroit way he had taken them in revealed their ignorance of the harsh world they were passing through, revealed how little they knew of the dangerous men who now inhabited that world. They still trusted another man. These, then, were from some sheltered place in the East, journeying westward to some point on the Mississippi. Or *across* the Mississippi. That sudden thought shocked him, stilled his fingers.

Their destination was on the other side of the river! Two trucks, each containing three men if he had judged correctly; two trucks and six men driving for the quarantine line, carrying with them their supplies and radiation suits to protect them while passing through contaminated territory. With smouldering excitement he slid the wheel off the hub and replaced it with the spare. Unscrewing the valve cap, he reversed it and jammed it down inside the valve as he let the jack drop the car. There was a faint whisper of escaping air.

He stood up. 'You want the jack back, Lieutenant?'

The man hesitated, struck by a new worry. He hadn't considered that complication before allowing Gary to work on the tyre and now he was unsure whether allowing him to handle it had somehow contaminated the tool. His face mirrored his uncertainty and he cursed himself for his shortsightedness. Finally he ordered, 'Put it in the back . . . easy now.'

'Yes, sir.' Gary went around to the rear and found the door opened for him. He peered into the darkened interior, found himself staring into the bore of the machine-gun. The gunner was seated on a packing case watching him, a cigarette hanging from his lips. The truck was loaded with similar wooden cases. Gary sniffed at the cigarette smoke.

'Toss it in,' the gunner said sharply.

'Okay, bud.' Gary dropped the jack on the nearest box and backed away, his eyes on the cigarette. The gunner reached out and closed the door.

'Well done, Corporal,' the lieutenant called. 'I shall mention this in my reports. You have been of valuable assistance to your government today.'

'Thank you, sir.' Gary's face was expressionless. 'The grub, Lieutenant?'

'Oh, yes.' He tossed out two boxes of C-rations. 'I'm sorry I can't give you more, but we are short. Just where are we, do you know?' He looked around as if expecting guideposts.

'Thank you, sir. This is Ohio – pretty close to the Indiana line. And Lieutenant, I wouldn't stay in any of the towns overnight – they'd probably gang up on you. Keep to the open country.'

'Thank you, Corporal. We've already found that sound advice. And now, don't recover your weapon until we are out of range.' He gunned the motor and put the truck into reverse gear, pulling it back on to the road. An impatient beat on the horn urged the other truck forward. 'Goodbye and good luck.'

The two vehicles rolled away.

Gary watched them go. 'So long, you scurvy sonofabitch.' The machine-gunner in the rear truck tossed a package of cigarettes through the broken window. Gary bent over to pick up the rations and turned to get the gun. When he straightened again the swiftly moving trucks were some distance away. He walked along the pavement, retrieved the cigarettes and stuffed them in an inner pocket. When the vehicles vanished from sight he quickly abandoned the road and took to the field, to follow. If he had guessed right on that leaking tyre, he should overtake the convoy when they stopped for the night.

The trucks were parked back-to-back in a small grove of trees. That would mean a machine-gunner sat in each cab, covering three avenues of approach. Gary studied the scene. They had stopped for the night in a small roadside park built and maintained by the state highway department, a stopping place originally installed for tourists. A gravel road curved off the highway and through the clump of green trees; there were two or three picnic tables that somehow had been overlooked in the search for firewood, a drinking fountain probably fed by a fresh-water spring, and a pair of rusty cans for trash. The gravelled path made room for a half dozen cars beneath the shading branches before completing the arc back to the highway. The trucks were but shapeless masses in the night; he might have missed them altogether had he been travelling along the paved road.

Gary waited in the underbrush on the far edge of the grove, wondering how to take the convoy.

They were green troops – they had allowed him to come this close undetected, but he knew they weren't so green as to permit him to simply walk up to the trucks. He had been lying at the edge of the grove for two hours, watching and waiting, and still he lacked a plan of action. Each cab held a man – they had betrayed themselves earlier and many times as they held matches to cigarettes. The flare of the matches revealed no other faces beside them, and although he could not be certain, he thought he could distinguish the shapes of men lying on the ground beneath the trucks. There may be one man in the rear of each vehicle, stretched out on the boxes. Maybe. If so, that left two on the ground.

He was still there, patiently waiting an unknown time later, when a noise from one of the trucks alerted him.

The sentry of one truck put his head out of the window and called back to the other cab. Although he kept his voice low, the words carried quite clearly.

'Hey – Jackson!'

'Yeah?' The second head appeared in the opposite cab.

'What time is it? My damned watch stopped.'

'Almost midnight.'

'That's close enough – let's wake these guys up and turn in.'

'I'm ready – damn' near asleep now.'

There was a scuffling noise from the interior of the nearer truck, and hushed voices in the other. Gary crept closer. The sentries changed places in the seats of the cab with noisy movement, awakening one of the figures on the ground. The man put his head out from under the truck and spoke sharply.

'What's going on up there?'

'Midnight, Lieutenant. Changing watch.'

'Well, be more quiet about it.'

'Yes, sir.'

The officer lay back on the ground, moved about as though

he were hunting the spot where he had been sleeping, and abruptly rolled from beneath the truck. He stood up.

'I'm going to take five. Keep your eyes open.'

'Yes, sir.'

The lieutenant walked towards the spot where Gary lay, fumbling with his clothes. Gary hugged the ground and let him approach, waited until the man paused beside a tree. He rose up silently and smoothly when the officer's hands were occupied, and reached for him.

After an interval Gary tautly stalked into the clearing and slid under the truck, ready to open fire if he were challenged. He rooted about on the grass, sighed, and lay still. Above him the newly awakened sentry scratched a match on the dashboard to light a cigarette. Gary hugged the lieutenant's automatic under his shirt and waited for time to pass. His first act was to eliminate the other sleeping man beside him, and two were out of the way.

It required another half-hour to reach the sentry sitting behind the wheel, a tedious half-hour of creeping along the rocky ground without noise, of hugging the side of the truck and raising his body towards the window sill. He held a pebble in his hand. When he was standing upright slightly to the rear of the open window, he tossed the pebble over the truck and heard it strike the ground beyond. Clutching the barrel of the automatic, he curled his left arm around and through the window to catch the sentry on the back of the head. He caught the man before he could slump forward into the horn, and lowered his body to the seat. There was no other sound, no movement from within or from the second vehicle.

Slowly and carefully he opened the door to let himself inside. The sentry of a short while before was sleeping soundly, and then he wasn't sleeping at all. There remained only the two in the other truck.

He needed information, needed it badly if he hoped to cross the river alive. After turning over the problem in his mind, he suddenly opened the door of the truck with no attempt at concealment, and climbed out to walk back to the other cab.

A head appeared before him. 'Keep quiet, dammit! You want the lieutenant on your tail?'

Gary rammed the automatic into his face. 'Come out of there, slow and clean.'

The face stared at him in the night, moved back to look down at the gun. 'For Ch – '

'Shut up and come out – now!'

The sentry scrambled out. 'Don't shoot!'

'Get your buddy out here. Make it fast.'

The sentry beat on the panel of the truck and after a moment a second face appeared in the open door. 'What the hell is – ' He stopped, staring.

'This is going on,' Gary retorted. 'Come on, outside.' He stood the two of them against the side of the truck, facing away from him, their hands atop their heads with fingers locked together. '*Now* you're going to give information or you're going to be dead ducks. Which is it going to be?'

'I don't know nothing.'

'You know where you're going,' Gary contradicted.

There was a moment of silent hesitation. The two exchanged glances.

Gary prodded one with the automatic. 'Where?'

'There's a bridge at a place called Fort Madison, Iowa,' the soldier told him sullenly. 'We – '

Gary chopped him short by reversing the gun and bringing the butt down on his head. The man crumpled to the ground. His companion stared down at the unconscious form.

'The bridge at Fort Madison,' Gary said smoothly, 'has a hole in it a mile wide. Now I'll ask you.' He stepped close to ram the barrel in the man's spine. 'Where are you going?'

'It ain't Fort Madison,' the other answered shakily. 'It's a bridge called the Chain of Rocks, or some name like that. It's around St. Louis someplace. They're waiting for us there.'

'Who is?'

'I don't know – honest I don't. The whole damned army, I guess. We're just supposed to deliver these trucks.'

'Why? What's in them?'

'Some gold. Gold bricks.'

'You're lying!'

'Hold it – I'm not! Go look for yourself if you don't believe me. We had three loads of that damned gold. We lost a truck back there in the mountains somewhere.'

'Lost it?'

'They jumped us – like those guys did today. The captain was in that one.'

'What in the hell does the army want that gold for?'

'I don't know. We just had orders to deliver it.'

Gary considered the matter, intently watching the man. 'The government must be getting hard up; three trucks started out, eh? You guys are pretty green – I'm surprised you got this far. How's everybody in Washington?'

The soldier half-turned to look at him. 'We ain't from Washington – we're outta Fort Knox.'

'For . . . ' Gary was instantly suspicious. 'Then what the hell you doing this far north?'

'I don't know, fella. I didn't write the orders. The lieutenant said we come this way and follow route 50. And we was doing just that.' He added bleakly, 'Until you enemy agents showed up.'

Gary let it pass. 'What happens next – when you deliver the trucks to the bridge?'

'Well, we just drive across and join 'em, I guess.'

'Did they say you could?' Gary held his breath.

'If we don't catch the plague. We was supposed to wear the monkey suits all the time, but the lieutenant said we didn't have to unless some of you ene . . . unless you guys bothered around. They're supposed to test us at the bridge and if we're clean, we can cross over.' He cast another backwards glance at Gary. 'Me, I'm damned glad you're healthy. I don't want no plague. Have you really been around since the bombing?'

Gary nodded. 'Couple of hundred miles south of Chicago when it happened.' He thought of another question. 'What happens now – with the lieutenant dead, I mean? Yeah – he's dead all right.' The soldier had twisted around to study the other truck, seeking his companions. 'All of them, except you and your buddy here – and he's in no condition to drive. What are you going to do now? *You*, I mean; what do the orders read?'

The soldier didn't answer at once. He stared at the side of

the truck some inches before his face and then looked down at the man lying at his feet. He seemed to take faint hope from the question.

'Damned if I know for sure,' he answered presently. 'The lieutenant was shooting off his mouth all the time – I got a hazy idea what to do. And he's carrying papers; he's got the captain's stuff, too. I guess the only thing to do is beat it for the bridge and tell them you – tell them what happened.'

'Can you make it by yourself?' Gary insisted. 'Can you get across without the officers? Know the password or the signal?'

'There ain't none that I heard of; we just stop in the middle of the bridge and wait for them to come out to us. I told you they've been waiting for us.'

Gary pursed his lips, relishing the simplicity of it. 'Are there any more coming? More trucks behind you?'

The soldier shook his head. 'Not yet, not until we get there okay. If we . . . I mean, if I make it, there'll be more on the way.'

'Is that a fact? This road will be crawling with them in no time at all.' He thoughtfully rubbed the stubble on his face, realising he had better shave again. 'Why the devil didn't they send a column to protect you? They should have known what to expect on this side of the river.'

He was answered by a bitter laugh. 'Corporal, there *ain't* no column to send. Most of our men got caught above ground and died in the plague – or deserted. *We've* been living down in the hole ever since . . . and I'll bet there ain't a hundred left. Hell, mister, we've got more trucks than we got men to drive them.' He lapsed into silence.

Gary backed away to glance about the grove, alert for sound or movement. Two trucks, loaded with gold ingots for a pinched government west of the Mississippi – and if these arrived safely, more to come. But two in the grove were worth a hundred others still at Knox, especially if this man should reach the river with his story. He came to a quick decision.

'I think,' he said slowly, 'that the lieutenant should go along; it might look better to show up with his body, just in case we are questioned. You'll find him over there in the trees.'

The soldier peered around at him warily.

Gary jerked the automatic. 'Go get him!' He stepped clear of the vehicle to cover the man. The trooper crossed the clearing to thrash among the underbrush and presently located the officer's body. Grunting, he carried it back to dump it in the rear of the truck, across the wooden boxes.

'Ready to roll? How about gas?'

The other nodded. 'Gassed up when we stopped. We carry our own.' And then he added, 'Pretty slick trick with that tyre.'

Gary's grin was lost in the darkness. 'You haven't seen anything yet. What about grub and ammo? Got plenty in both trucks?'

'Yeah. In case we got separated.'

'If I helped myself to one of the trucks, could you get along all right in the other one?'

'Sure. Say, are you thinking of . . . ?'

'Never mind what I'm thinking. And you'd better be telling the truth because your life may depend on it. I'm pulling out of here with this one. How's that for slickness?'

'You'll never get across . . . ' He stopped, and then began again. 'What for? The lieutenant's in there.'

'The lieutenant will take me across. And listen to some good advice, bud – the old voice of experience himself. I've lived two years in this damned country, and if you hope to live that long you'll have to keep your eyes and ears open, and shoot first. Don't pull any more damned fool tricks like you did tonight – and if I was you, I'd head south this fall. Got all that?'

'You can't get away with it! I'll follow you to the river and tell them – '

Gary rammed his face close and laughed. 'You can follow me all you please, but you won't tell them nothing! You don't seem to get the idea, bud. You're an enemy agent, *now*.' And he clipped him with a short, hard right.

Gary rolled his body aside, and then strode back to the second truck. Lifting the hood, he ripped out the distributor cap and pocketed it and then to satisfy his mounting excitement he tore loose the wiring to the plugs and smashed the glass gasoline cup. He tried to take off the fan belt but it resisted his fingers. Dropping the hood, he reached under the truck and hauled out the dead man lying there. This one, of the party of six, was nearest his height and build. He stripped the body of its uniform and as an afterthought, removed the chain and dog tags from the man's neck.

Gary shoved aside the body of the lieutenant to examine the contents of the truck he had chosen. There were three radiation suits, the machine-gun, several dozen boxes of C-rations, red gasoline cans and the personal effects of the troopers. Satisfied, he seated himself behind the wheel.

Without lights, the truck left the roadside park and rolled on to the highway, nose to the west.

Somewhere in Illinois, Gary stopped the vehicle on a deserted highway and climbed out, cradling the machine-gun. Walking a distance from the truck, he turned and spewed it with slugs, leaving it nicked and scarred as though it had undergone a running battle. Taking off his clothes, he threw away his own identification tags and slipped the stolen chain over his head. His new name, he learned, was Forrest Moskowitz. He read the serial number over several times, striving to memorise the initial four or five digits. Satisfied, he put on the uniform. The papers carried by the late captain and lieutenant were already familiar to him – as the sole survivor, he would be expected to have read them from curiosity if nothing else. Gary was confident he could carry his new identity smoothly. There remained only the odd chance that someone at or near the bridge was familiar with Fort Knox.

He clothed the lieutenant's body in a radiation suit, donned another himself, and drove on.

The truck neared the Chain of Rocks bridge.

Two years – nearly two years since the day of his thirtieth birthday, the day of a glorious drunk and personal disaster. Two years since awakening in that broken-down hotel to find dust on the bed and death everywhere in the city. Two years since he had moved among living people with no great fear of the present or the future. Two years of dodging, hiding, stealing, killing to eat and stay alive, two years of hunting or be hunted. How many dead men lay behind him, he wondered then? How many lives had he taken to protect his own, or to gain what he wanted?

He couldn't remember their number.

But to hell with all that, to hell with the memories and the hunger and the freezing cold. Ahead lay the bridge.

He approached it slowly and cautiously, turned on to the span and commenced the long climb to the middle of the river, the truck creeping along at less than twenty miles per hour. A knot of excited panic gripped his stomach and for a brief moment he debated turning back, abandoning the truck and the sighted goal to turn and flee for the comparative safety of a known ground. Gary fought it away and drove on. Just over the arbitrary dividing line, just past that invisible point where the Illinois boundary touched Missouri, two tanks waited for him in the roadway, blocking passage with their bulk.

He pulled up short, staring into their gun muzzles. They excited him, frightened him not a little and at the same time they appealed to an almost forgotten emotion within him. *Now* he was standing under their snouts with impunity, in safety, and they again imparted the peculiar sense of friendly guns facing a common enemy. *His* guns now – almost. He climbed from the truck to lift an arm in greeting but they did not reply. Gary leaned against the vehicle to await their next move. He wanted desperately to smoke but the suit prevented it.

After a while he heard a car come racing up the other side of the bridge. It came to a skidding halt just beyond the tanks and several clothed figures emerged, clumsily grasping hand weapons. They moved around the tanks and advanced upon him. Gary held his position, nervously alert but striving to hide any fear of them. When they were but ten feet distant the group stopped and a leader motioned with his arm. Gary obeyed by moving away from the truck, to lean on the bridge railing and watch.

The suited troopers closed in on the truck, yanking open the rear door to examine the interior and kneeling to peer underneath. They found the body of the lieutenant – with obvious surprise, the precious cargo, Gary's hijacked supplies and nothing more. Again the anonymous leader motioned and two of the troopers climbed into the truck to roll it forward across the state line. Heavy motors broke into sudden, noisy life as one of the tanks moved sluggishly aside. The truck shot past it, and the tank resumed its former position.

The remaining troops herded Gary forward.

They marched around the tanks and at an unspoken command, Gary climbed into the waiting automobile with the others pushing in behind him. The car turned about, jockeying back and forth on the bridge to return to the Missouri shore. The nearer faces in the seat peered at him curiously. The car shot forward. Gary slumped against the back of the seat, exhausted with tension. He was in! After two years of bitter struggle and constant dreaming, he had realised his ambition and crossed the river.

CHAPTER ELEVEN

An ornate brick building flashed past his window, a building which had housed the toll-collector's offices back before a part of the world had ended; now it contained a command post with a pair of sentries before the door. They stared at the passing car, watched after it when it pulled up before a smaller and newer building a short distance down the road.

At a pressure on his arm, Gary left the car and followed the troopers towards the small building. Someone opened the steel door, pushed him in and then crowded in after him. The door was slammed and bolted from the inside. The leader made some sort of a signal and an instant later the whole ceiling seemed to open, showering down on them a thick grey fog. Gary jerked back nervously, fighting the swirling mist with ineffective fists. The man nearest him seized his arms, held him still, and then thumped his back encouragingly. At that moment he realised what it was, where he was – this was the decontamination chamber, erected to cleanse the troops returning from patrols. Or returning from the task of throwing bodies over the bridge rails.

The fog closed around him, hiding the others.

After an interval he detected a new note in the chamber and the mist began to dissipate as blowers sucked the gas away. The other men began peeling off their suits. He lifted a slow hand to open his, and was stopped.

'Hold it, buddy. Not yet. You've gotta be processed, so keep it on until we get out of here.'

Now what the devil did he mean by that? Gary watched them, the nervous knot again forming in his stomach. They slid out of their suits and left the building, slamming the door behind them to leave him standing there alone. Again he raised a hand and commenced undressing, noticing for the first time that his uniform didn't quite fit him, that he had a stubble of beard. Abruptly the steel door opened and a medical corpsman appeared there.

He stared at Gary professionally. 'I oughtta get a medal for this,' the man announced briskly. 'Maybe you got the plague.'

'And maybe I haven't!' Gary retorted. 'Come on, get it over with. I want to get outside – this place gives me the willies.'

'You don't go outside, brother – not until your tests come out. Gimme your arm.'

'The hell I don't! What for?'

'The hell you don't.' The soldier reached for his arm. 'Blood tests, see? You might be carrying something. We gotta be damned careful.' He plunged the needle in Gary's arm and drew forth a sample. 'What type blood?'

'How do I know?' Gary said with angry impatience.

'By looking at your tag, stupid.' He reached out a swift hand to lift the chain hanging from Gary's neck, to read the inscription on the metal tag. '*AB*. Kinda rare, ain't you?'

'What do you mean by that crack?'

'*AB* ain't common around here chum, like in the Egyptians or the Chinese maybe.' He glanced at the tag again. 'You're Moskowitz, huh? Well, I've seen funnier – maybe you're an Egyptian Moskowitz.'

'Get the hell out of here!' Gary was fast losing his temper, aided by a growing fear. 'And bring me something to eat – I'm damned tired of C-rations.'

'Okay, okay.' The corpsman completed his work and left.

Gary sat down on the floor to wait and to brood. He waited a full hour, worrying about the dog tag on his neck. The stolen Moscowitz tag – and the Moscowitz blood type. He hadn't thought about that. It occurred to him suddenly that he hadn't thought about many things, little things really that seemed unimportant until they reached out to push him before a firing squad. What were they doing with the lieutenant's body? He had strangled the man and later encased the body in a radiation suit, but there were no bullet holes in the suit. What did *that* do to his carefully prepared story of ambush, with himself the only survivor?

The personnel from Knox were not supposed to remove their suits on the journey, but they had done so, believing themselves safe from contamination so long as they did not fraternise with 'enemy agents'. If then he admitted that the lieutenant had removed his suit en route and had been strangled by an enemy, it followed that Gary must have replaced the suit after the officer was dead. It also followed that both the officer and Gary had exposed themselves to the plague. That would be the certain end of *him*. On the other hand it was difficult to believe that the lieutenant could be strangled while wearing his suit – and there was the manufactured evidence of a bullet-scarred truck to show that the ambushers had used guns, not fingers to kill.

Bitterly, he realised he should have left the rotting officer behind. Rotting . . . the thought took form, shaped itself into a faint hope. It might be that they would not remove the suit from the lieutenant's body.

There were other things – he didn't know the names of the people of Knox, he didn't know the history or background of Moskowitz . . . didn't so much as know the man's enlistment date. The serial numbers on the dog tag would give some clue to that, but he couldn't guess the accurate answers from the numbers. His only chance of escaping detection there lay in the fact that serial records may have been destroyed in a ravaged Washington.

The door opened and the corpsman entered, carrying a tray.

'Another medal – you phony Egyptian!'

'I ain't no Egyptian,' Gary flared, half frightened.

'I'll say you ain't. *AB* hell! You ain't no more *AB* than I am. In case anybody asks, you're a big fat round *O*. Better remember that – you might need it sometime.'

'But the tag says –'

'The tag lies like a rug, chum, but don't let it throw you. You're an early bird, ain't you?' He put down the tray. 'It happened all the time, back at the beginning; they rushed them through fast and made some mistakes. I'll bet one guy out of every twenty is walking around with the wrong type on his tag – or pushing up flowers. Sloppy work, but you can't help it.

Only trouble is, if you ever need a transfusion in a hurry and they pump the wrong kind into you – bingo.'

'Maybe it changed,' Gary suggested. 'It was a long time ago.'

'Nope.' The soldier shook his head and grinned at Gary's ignorance. 'It never changes, no more than fingerprints. You was born with *O* and you'll die with *O*. Now eat up. I'll bring in water and a can pretty soon; you're stuck here until the tests prove out. Two or three days maybe.'

'What for?' he asked again. 'Why the tests?'

'To see if you picked up anything, stupid. If you're carrying any plague germs around, we'll soon know it.' He backed away. 'And I'll earn that damned medal.'

'That's a hell of a note. Listen – do me a favour. Put in for a pass for me. I've been out of circulation too long.'

'A pass he wants yet!'

Gary didn't get the pass – he never waited for it, never waited out the three days. He knew with certainty what those tests would reveal, knew beyond doubt that the test tubes or whatever things they used would point to his two years of wandering around the quarantined land, would shout what must be in his blood. Freedom was too near to wait three days.

He did nothing the first night, other than lie in the decontamination chamber and wait quietly. He called for and received repeated trays of food, a great quantity of water, the needed things a half-starved man would demand. And he noted with each opening and closing of the door that it was not locked from without. A single sentry stood outside, seldom at attention. They did not consider him a dangerous risk. Twice during the first night he sent out for water and once asked for more cigarettes. The sentry brought them, laid them in the doorway and retreated a few paces. Gary opened the door and hauled the things inside.

On the second day the medical corpsman brought paper and pencil and commenced questioning; he began in the routine way with Gary – or Moskowitz's immediate and current history, but quickly moved on to the journey made by the three truckloads of gold, and what happened to them. Gary hid his relief and spun an acceptable story. He included a vivid description of the country through which he had supposedly passed, and for spite threw in mention of the thousands of people they had seen, people hospitable and otherwise.

The questioner's head jerked up in disbelief. 'Huh?'

'Huh, what?' It seemed that Gary had him hooked.

'Thousands of enemy agents?'

'I don't know if they were enemy agents or not,' Gary said casually, 'but there were thousands of them all right. I don't mean in the cities – all the cities are dead and bombed out, we avoided those, but the little towns are full of people. Every time we passed through a whistle stop the whole damned population rushed out to greet us – just like those towns in France I went through.'

'But there *can't* be people over there, our people. They're all dead.'

Gary stared at him. 'Why should I lie about it?'

'Well – I dunno.'

'All right. The burgs are full, believe me. Farmers in the field – a lot of the horses are dead, I guess, because I saw men pulling ploughs.' He hid a grin, watching the corpsman write down what he had said. The corpsman would do more than that – he would spread it around the camp. He went on with his story, bringing it up to the point where the ambush had wiped out everyone but him and the lieutenant – and the lieutenant had died a few hours later. And say – did the lieutenant get a military funeral?

'Hell, no,' the corpsman answered. 'They weighted his body and dumped it in the river – ain't taking no chances.'

That night, the second in the chamber, Gary escaped.

He first considered asking the sentry for milk, knowing that milk would take longer to procure, but then quickly abandoned the idea with the knowledge that the sentry might well refuse – also being aware of the difficulty. Or if he did consent to go after it he might lock the door before leaving, or he might not be gone more than five minutes at the most. Five minutes were not enough. He needed hours to be free of the area.

Instead, Gary made the usual request for water and held the door opened the slightest crack, peering into the night. He could hear no one else near by, could smell no tobacco smoke in the air. The sentry returned with the water and stooped to place it on the doorsill – stiffening with surprise when his eyes noticed the tiny crack in the opening. Gary caught him on the back of the neck, cracking the side of his hand on the man's spinal cord. The sentry slumped. Gary thrust his head outside warily but there was no outcry. Quickly then he dragged the inert body into the chamber and stretched it out along the far wall where he had slept the night before. Within seconds he had slipped outside and locked the door behind him, to vanish instantly into the surrounding darkness, away from the river.

He counted on three to four hours. At least three hours before the guard was scheduled to be relieved.

He was wearing civilian clothes, a pair of dirty overalls and a nondescript sweater he had taken from a farmer. A couple of dollars in change, also belonging to the throttled farmer, rattled around in his pocket. The farmer's unconscious body lay many miles behind in a ditch but his ancient Ford truck sped along a highway to the south. Sunrise found Gary and the stolen truck nearly fifty miles south of St. Louis and well away from the river, well outside the ten-mile military zone.

This was freedom, this was what he had waited two years to see again.

He bowled along the highway at top speed, watching the unhurried activity about the farms, the sleepy beginnings of a new day in each small town he passed. There were no suspicious faces turned his way, no armed men to greet him at the village limits, no skulking figure to waylay the noisy truck as it sped along the road. This was free country, living country. Far behind him, unknown to him, not everything was so alive. A sentry lay dead in a decontamination chamber and a medical corpsman lay dying on a hospital bed, his body turning blue. Early alarm had turned to furore when the corpsman was discovered, and a hasty quarantine had been thrown around the camp guarding the bridge. Of a sudden two paramount problems had arisen for the responsible brass: finding the escaped carrier, and disposing of a few hundred men suddenly turned 'enemy agents'.

Finding Gary would be the easier of the two: he would mark his own trail.

Early that afternoon he entered a theatre and sat through a double feature, suddenly discovering as he passed the theatre that capering images had been one of the things he hungered for. The double feature consisted first of a very sexy woman flinging her body around in a bathing suit, to the dismay . . . and delight . . . of every other male and female in the picture; and next of the true-blue western hero throwing the deep-dyed villain for a loss to save the ranch. Each held him enthralled and he stayed for a second showing of the bathing suit, to emerge finally with another thought in mind. The idea wasn't so readily fulfilled, but he managed it by nightfall. His money was short, not nearly enough to eat and drink with, much less satisfy his desires. The first robbery netted him only pocket change, the second brought him a wallet. He left the town behind him and sought another.

He bought other clothes, not new ones for fear they would mark him, but second-hand garments in a shop. The farm truck was abandoned on a side street and he caught a bus, to find himself in Little Rock late that night. Little Rock held much of what he sought. Little Rock also held radios that blared forth the news, or part of the news of what had happened. An enemy agent was loose west of the river. He sat in a bar and listened to the bulletins repeated every fifteen minutes.

There was an interest in the bulletins, faces turned and ears listened, but after each one the faces went back to their preoccupations. There was talk, speculation, idle threats as to what *they* would do to the sonofabitch if he came *here*, but their most immediate interest lay in the liquor at hand and the companion at the table.

'Hell,' Gary told the bartender, 'he'll never get this far. The soldiers will catch him.'

The bartender agreed. 'They always do. Them soldiers are all right joes – I'm for 'em. They certainly changed things around here. You know what this state was before the change.'

Gary didn't, but nodded as if he did. He guessed that the bartender might be referring to the subject nearest his heart – the liquor trade – but he didn't dare reveal his ignorance by asking. He couldn't recall having been in Arkansas before, nor did he remember anything said about the place. Furthermore he didn't give a damn.

He left the establishment and wandered along the street, watching the neon lights and the blinking electric signs. Those too he had missed, longed for without stopping to think about it, and their brilliant flickerings fell across his eyes like memories. There weren't many cars, due to the petrol rationing, but the sounds of those passing was sweet on his ears, and even though the odour of burnt petrol stung his nostrils as he stepped from behind a bus, he liked it. This was living in the way he wanted to live. This was living again.

It wasn't hard to find a girl willing to share the contents of the wallet with him. She cooked breakfast for him the following morning and he was so delighted with the process and the deep sense of contentment, with the feeling of being at home with her – despite the shabby apartment and her lack of taste in dress and speech – that he asked to stay a few days. She was more than willing. She made a transparent kind of love to him that satisfied his long starvation diet – love that did not wait on an hour or a place; he tried to read her newspapers but she would interrupt, he fingered a few of her worn books but she plucked them from his hands and threw them across the room. She did not fool him – he knew it would stop when the wallet was empty, but meanwhile the wallet was not empty and she was a pleasing torrent after a two-year drought. He rumpled the false blonde hair and let her have her way.

He did not think to switch on the radio because now that he was *here*, what people said on the air *here* did not arouse curiosity or desire within him; and because her continual chatter was all that he desired in human speech at the moment. Hers was a friendly voice and a loving one; it satisfied him. So he did not hear the later bulletins and did not know the new tone the broadcasts had taken.

Gary spent a lazy, spendthrift afternoon walking about the city and buying things he both did and didn't need. For once the advertisements didn't annoy him and he purchased a new razor because a colourful sign told him he could be a smoother rooster; he found no Mother Mahaffey Candy Kitchen, but bought a box of chocolates for the girl waiting at the apartment. Stopping at half a dozen stores, loading his arms with groceries only for the pleasure of buying things, Gary wandered back to the apartment just before sunset. He twisted the knob with his fingers and shoved open the door with one knee, his voice raised to shout for the woman. Gary stopped short in the doorway to stare at the twisted, writhing body on the floor. She was clad only in a slip, her reddish-purple body ugly with approaching asphyxiation. She raised an accusing finger at him, trying to gasp out a few words. Behind her the radio was talking. He dropped the bundles from his arms and turned to run, forgetting even to close the door in his hasty flight.

Another bus, still southward because it was the first one out of the city.

He thought he had been in Shreveport before but he couldn't be sure – that other life had been so long ago that the memories of it sometimes played tricks on him. He might have been there a decade before with the Louisiana war games, or it may have been only a troop train passing through. But the memory of that tortured girl on the floor was no vague trick. It would not leave him, despite his efforts to wipe it away. It remained with him during the tedious bus ride south, haunted him as he stalked the brilliantly lit streets of Shreveport, a memory which burned bright and bitter. She lay on the floor, twisted, struggling for breath, accusing him with a barbed finger.

He couldn't stay anywhere now, couldn't stay longer than a day. Just one day! Wherever he paused, small town or bustling city, overnight at some farmhouse, he could stay but one day or his past would overtake him. That farm family – the Hoffmans – had not been affected by his presence for the same reasons they had lived through the initial exposure. They were immune, he was immune. These people living west of the river were not, and he was killing them. Carrying death to the people in the bus, the stores, those he jostled on the streets, the bartender, the girl in the shabby apartment.

Shreveport had lost the magic it once had known

He drank by himself, off in a corner as though a few empty tables would erect a wall between him and the others, ate at a small and nearly deserted restaurant that served him cheap unsatisfactory food. At the opposite end of the counter a taxi driver nursed a cup of coffee, dawdling over a newspaper. Gary turned his eyes away from the paper – there was no picture of him, they didn't have that, but he knew after one glance the headlines concerned him. With that paper, there were many more men than soldiers after him now. Everyone was watching for him. Some of them would see him, but not know him until it was too late. Damn that schoolteacher! He had called the turn with an accurate deadliness.

This then was the brightly glowing life he had wanted west of the river, life filled with women, food and drink that could not be had in the contaminated area. This was what he had risked his life to gain – and he could stay here one day.

'They'll get the bastard all right!'

Gary jerked around, brought his attention on the cabby. 'Yeah,' he said. 'Sure.' He put down money on the counter and walked out.

So he was a bastard to be hunted and shot, simply because he wanted to live with them instead of in that empty wasteland to the east. They wanted to kill him because he should have died long ago and didn't – wanted to kill him if they could find him. The laugh was on them. He actually held them in the hollow of his hand; he had only to cough in the cab driver's face, to touch or kiss the waitress, to throw his arm about the shoulders of a drunken barfly and he could slay them while they were hunting him. But he could stay only one day. Tomorrow they would discover he had been there.

Had been there. The taxi stood at the kerb, motor running.

Gary turned his head to look back through the restaurant window, to see the cabby still buried in his paper. The girl was bringing him a second coffee. Gary stepped off the kerb and walked around the vehicle to slide under the wheel. He released the brake and put the car into low gear, moving off slowly and quietly to avoid attention of the driver. When he was a block away he changed gears and pushed the throttle to the floor, scooting along the nearly deserted street. A cross-town thoroughfare claimed his attention and he turned west, thinking to flee still further from the river. By this time those trailing him would believe him going steadily south.

He found the western route closed. A roadblock had been thrown across the highway and two or three cars were lined up there, undergoing an inspection by uniformed police. Without changing speed he turned off on a side road and drove north, striving to give the impression such had been his route.

He continued north until he came to an intersecting road, and pivoted towards the city once more. Back in Shreveport he directed the cab south, having described a complete circle from his earlier start, only to find a similar roadblock on the highway to Alexandria and Baton Rouge. He stopped well back from the barrier where police were inspecting the passengers of a cross-country bus, and turned around.

The routes to the west and south were closed to him – the plague scare had snowballed that quickly to those dimensions. Escape to the north might be open, on the theory that he would not return that way, but again he would find barriers thrown up on the southern outskirts of Little Rock. The girl lay on the apartment floor in Little Rock – the last apparent clue to him. There would be more in Shreveport tomorrow or the next day. A waitress, another bartender, more . . .

Escape only to the east?

Driving cautiously, Gary sent the cab across the Red River into Bossier City. No one stopped him. He continued on, seeking out and finding the federal route to Monroe and the Mississippi. There were no roadblocks that way. Not yet.

Not yet . . . but there would be soon. As soon as that cab-driver reported his stolen vehicle, as soon as the police manning the roadblocks reported the cab had not gone west or south. Suddenly the cab stuck out like a yellow thumb on a bare highway. He had to get rid of it.

The opportunity came shortly after dawn next morning.

She was a middle-aged woman driving an old Model A Ford, driving it slowly and carefully along her lane. Gary slowed the stolen cab and fell in behind her, watching the manner of her driving, noting that her speed never exceeded a steady, careful thirty miles an hour. A cautious, lonely woman driving in a lonely dawn, intent on some distant destination. She had pulled over on the far right side of the road to permit him to pass, and was taking quick peeks at the cab in her mirror.

Gary shoved down on the accelerator and shot around her, to swing directly in front of the Ford and apply the brakes. She obediently slowed, nervously gauging her distance by watching his bumper and tail-lights. He slackened speed again, dropping well below her accustomed thirty and was satisfied to see the uncertainty on her face. She tried to fall well behind him but he kept his foot on the brake and stayed just ahead of her. Finally, when the two vehicles were doing less than ten miles an hour, he jerked to a complete stop. Her reflexes were not quick enough and the Ford piled into the rear of the cab.

Gary slid out from under the wheel, leaving the motor running and the door open, to walk back and inspect the damage. She was beside him in an instant, berating him for his poor driving and decrying the damage to her own car. Without a word he seized her arm and pulled her forward, to place her on the front seat of the cab. She stared at him, speechless then with surprise and growing anger. He left her there, ran back to the Ford and jumped in. Before she could recover her wits and step down to the pavement he had backed the Ford away from the tangle of bumpers and shot forward, curving out and around the stalled cab with a rich burst of speed. The woman screamed at him as he sped by. The old car would do no more than fifty, wide open, but he slammed his foot to the boards and held it there until the yellow taxi and wildly gesticulating woman had fallen from sight.

Gary slowed to a leisurely thirty, secure in the belief that the cautious woman would not attempt to close the gap between them. Plus the necessary amount of time she would need before continuing in the cab – she would undoubtedly waste many minutes, debating the honesty of driving off in the strange vehicle.

The high-pitched sound of a diving plane caught his ear. Gary twisted the wheel and savagely nosed the car over into the nearer ditch, to leap clear and run for the fields as soon as the Ford had come to rest. At the fence he stopped. The plane was several miles behind him, back along the highway he had just traversed and it was not coming his way. He wandered back to the road, staring into the distance.

The aircraft's motors were screaming again and he found it just as it was pulling out of a dive. As he watched, the plane climbed into the sky, snapped around in another circling approach, and dived at the highway once more. Quite clearly he could hear the rattle of machine-guns. The ship plummeted below the horizon and was hidden for only a moment, before tilting its nose for the climb. It made one last pass at the target while Gary stood there watching, and then stayed in the sky to aimlessly circle the object, waiting.

The cabdriver would be annoyed at the loss of his vehicle.

Gary backed the Ford on to the road and hurried eastward towards the river, towards the only place of safety that he knew. He hoped the occupants of the plane would not notice his car. There was no shred of doubt *now* that his presence had been detected in Shreveport.

The river lay wide and dark ahead of him, moving along listlessly with a whispering nothing that wasn't quite sound and yet was not silence. The real silence lay on the other side, a silence so complete it was a tangible thing that could be held in the hand. A loud, hurtful silence. Gary lay motionless, frozen in the marshy grasses, his eyes searching for the black silhouette of a sentry against the night sky. They knew he was here somewhere now, knew that he had entered the forbidden ten-mile zone, knew with certainty that he was hiding in some secret place between the wrecked taxi and the river. They even knew where he was going, and would have denied him the right to go back to the silence.

Gary lay still, hating the silence and the river.

There was no other choice for him if he wanted to go on living beyond this moment and this hour, and that knowledge angered him. He felt a burning hatred of the choice, of the narrowness of it and of the hard necessity for making it. He could spring to his feet now and shout his defiance of the west – to die in the next second, or he could go back across the line of quarantine – and what? The river was a tormenting barrier that divided the nation in halves, unequal halves in which unequal lives were played out on a stage of poverty or plenty. For many – food, drink, chocolates, radio, sensation, gasoline, money, neon, flesh, sleep, peace. For some – be quick or be dead, starve slowly or die quickly by violence. And so common a thing as a river was the line of bitter division.

The black and almost shapeless mass of a prowling sentry moved against the stars.

Gary stopped breathing, watching the dim figure stalk past him, watching him out of sight. He counted a hundred while waiting for any others that might be following the sentry and then rose up on hands and knees to edge towards the water. A rock turned under his knee and he froze to the sand, watching and listening. Slowly then, feeling his way with his senses as much as his fingers, he wormed towards the river's edge, on the alert for trip wires. One outstretched hand came down in water, causing a minute splash. After a taut, silent moment of listening he lowered his naked body into the river and moved sluggishly away from the Louisiana shore.

He swam for one of the tiny spits of land he had seen in midstream while reconnoitring in the early evening, swam and floated for any of the islands that would give him a brief rest before pushing on to the silence beyond. The hatred still churned within him, hatred now for his own bitter futility and silly hopes that he could live like a man again. Hatred for the injustice that had been done him after two years of watchful waiting and crafty planning; he had succeeded in crossing the forbidden river only to have his triumph hurled in his face, and now he was literally crawling back again with nothing left to him but his life, a naked and defenceless body returning to the dead silence.

He pushed on, increasing the bite of his strokes.

For a flashing instant he wished he could have spread the disease beyond stopping, could have run free through hundreds of towns and villages spewing a choking death as he ran. He wished he could have pulled the smug and stupid western states down to his own level by carrying the plague to the mountains, could have shown them what really lay on the eastern side of the river.

Gary paddled on in the darkness until he felt a mixture of

mud and sand beneath his feet. Pulling himself out of the water, he got to his feet and turned to shake an angry fist at the Louisiana shore.

'You sonsabitches!'

The farm woman in the riddled taxi would have appreciated that; the anonymous man whose body had been hurled into the frozen creek might even have grinned with the humour of it. Clumsy Harry, in his ignorant haste to crawl the cable, would have laughed out loud.

CHAPTER TWELVE

The long sparse sliver of land jutted out into the blue-green waters of the Gulf, tiny swells running up to foam on the baking sandy beach. That alone had not changed. The Florida sun was hot and uncomfortable in midsummer.

Gary pawed through the charred remains of the old fisherman's cabin, seeking some slight clue to the fate of its occupants, something to indicate how long ago they had departed – and in what manner. He wanted desperately to know how long ago the familiar shack had burned to the ground.

He walked along the glaring white shore-line and stared out to sea, remembering how he and Oliver had fished there, how Sally had watched a sail which was quite invisible to them beating across the Gulf. Their old mail truck was gone, vanished completely with no remaining sign of how it had left. The ruins of the cabin still held the cooking stove, a mass of wrecked and useless metal now that was rapidly rusting away; that and some miscellaneous scrap which had not survived the fire in any recognisable form. A part of the wooden causeway to the mainland had been broken up and carried away, or burned on the spot. Other parts of it sagged with rotten, collapsing timbers. The wind, the rain and the water had destroyed all traces of human passage other than his own fresh footprints.

Oliver was gone, Sally gone – the baby gone. Where?

He kicked angrily at the charred wood and realised that the initial advantage of wintering here was no longer an advantage – it had now become a definite, deadly liability. Too many of the survivors were moving down from the North to escape the punishing winters, too many of them had discovered the warm sands and the seas filled with food. He knew that those who still survived *this* year were the deadliest, the hard core of a savage, steady, dwindling life east of the Mississippi. He stopped pacing to count and frown. *This* year was . . . what?

The fifth year? Five years since the bombs fell? In which of those years, then, had strangers found the tiny cabin, sacked it, burned it?

His bare foot came down on an artificial something which dug into his skin and he bent over to examine it, pry it from the sands which half buried it. The wooden link chain he had carved and given to Sally . . . for Christmas, one of those years ago.

Abruptly, Gary quit the island, conscious of his exposed position.

CHAPTER THIRTEEN

He had to find something to eat.

Three days without food were racking his stomach with pain, causing his guts to rumble and ache. The air of the cave was foul and dead from his refuse, blurring his wits and creating a dangerous drowsiness. A bucket for drinking water in the rear of the cave contained a scant half-inch of liquid – he could make that stretch another day if need be, but he had to have something to eat soon. The last of the few edible roots he had ripped from the frozen ground were gone and if he delayed longer, he would be too weak and dulled to fight.

Gary picked up his .22 rifle and crawled to the mouth of the cave to search the snow-covered plain.

In earlier years he had favoured the shotgun or the heavier rifle, along with many men who wanted or needed the greater distance and more powerful shell. But other men who clung stubbornly to those heavier rifles were no longer alive. The crack of a heavy rifle carries a long distance – too long a distance across the silent, watchful land. The crack of a gun meant *man*, and a man fired only to bring down food. He had quickly discovered what a smaller gun could do, discovered that it carried a far less betraying noise but, if he were near enough, could bring down a man just as easily. Gary let the other hunters with heavy rifles stalk the game and reveal their presence – and then eliminated them with the .22. There was so little food to be had that no one hesitated to close another mouth.

The plain before him was clear, white and bright with fresh-fallen snow. Nothing moved across his vision.

He carefully parted the brush and wriggled through the mouth of the cave, pausing every few inches to look and listen and sniff the air. The hillside was barren of life or movement as he emerged into the open, and he rose to his knees the better to search the field below and the rising slope of the hill behind him. A man had very nearly killed him there, three or four years before. The man had lain for days above the cave mouth waiting for him to emerge, slashing down with a rusted bayonet as his head and neck protruded through the opening. His only mistake was that he was too slow, his long hunger robbing his mind and muscles of concerted action. Gary caught the hand that held the bayonet and yanked him down. Afterwards he strung the hill with concealed wires.

Moving guardedly down the hill, he paused to look back at his revealing tracks in the snow. They disclosed his hiding-place, advertised his presence, but there was nothing he could do about it now. It would mean the use of extra caution when returning to the cave, but meanwhile the snow would also reveal an intruder. Snow usually brought into the open what few rabbits that remained, snow betrayed the tracks and trails of chipmunk, grey squirrel, field mice – anything edible. He set traps when he could; ammunition was scarce, valuable. He had managed to loot and steal barely enough to last him through the winter.

At the base of the hill Gary settled down against the white frozen ground, unmoving, listening, his taut nostrils held to the wintry air. There was nothing, no one beside himself. A part of him hungered for the past when there had been others, other men and women moving around without danger to themselves so long as they took reasonable precautions. He liked to remember a winter and a farmhouse in Wisconsin, a family who lived in the old familiar way, a radio, a little girl. And three meals a day. That had been a long time ago, many years ago when he was younger and ate more regularly than he did now. *Now* he counted himself fortunate when he had something to eat two or three times in the same week and *now* that enforced hunger was leaving its marks on his body. *Now* he bitterly resented a competing mouth, and that other mouth resented his.

The snowy plain remained empty and silent, dead. An old concrete highway crossed the middle of it, crumbling away.

There had been but one car on that highway in the past . . .

how many years? Perhaps ten? How long had it been since he had awakened in that dimly remembered hotel to find the world poisoned around him? How long since the winter on the Florida beach, that other winter in the Wisconsin farmhouse, the brief, unhappy excursion across the Mississippi into the land of the living? All of ten years, surely. But there had been a car creeping along that vacant highway since then, since he had taken to living in the cave. A heavily armoured truck that reminded him of the mail truck, that rumbled through the valley searching for someone, anyone. The noise of the approaching motor had excited him, made him want to rush down to it, but common sense forced him to hide in the brush and watch it pass. It finally vanished into the distant afternoon sunlight and had not come back.

There was nothing on the plain. He stood up from his cramped position and slowly moved around the base of the hill, rifle at the ready.

A brook, doubtless frozen now, wound among the rocks on the far side of the hill and that was his immediate goal, for animals – and sometimes men – stopped there to drink. A few scattered trees gave scant cover as he neared it and he dropped to his belly, searching the area for tracks. There would be no man-tracks here, only those of animals. A man would have smelled the promised snow the night before, would have lain up on the hillside to observe the water hole or would have hidden himself in the trees overhead.

Gary could see nothing among the trees and directed his eyes towards the hill, raising his nostrils to the air. There were no tell-tale odours; ground and wind alike were bare. Approaching the frozen stream, he studied the snow but it was smooth and without marks. There was no game there.

In the far distance a gun boomed, vibrating the air.

Startled, surprised and yet pleased, he dropped quickly to the ground and searched the horizon.

It had been a medium rifle of some kind – the sound was too far off for easy identification. They had not been aware of him, else they wouldn't have fired at that distance. The thought of someone else near by, of possible food there for the taking, quickened the pangs of hunger in his stomach. He waited only long enough to scan the fields around and behind him, to see if another man had heard the shot and was moving to investigate, before leaping to his feet. Gary set off at a fast trot for the white horizon, the world empty about him.

The sound of the gun had seemed to come from somewhere near the town – always a deadly trap.

Men still loved towns, were still fascinated by them, still dreamed of them. Uncautious men sometimes visited the towns and died in them – the prey of others who waited there and waylaid them. A few who were wiser, more experienced like Gary, often waited outside the towns for the unwary visitor and stopped them in their tracks before they could enter. Once they entered they fared no better. But sometimes a town was actually empty and remained that way because men in the vicinity only thought there were others within.

Two hours of moving swiftly across the snow brought Gary near the town. Suddenly there, he found the new trail.

He crouched down again, making himself a small and almost unnoticeable hump in the snow as he studied the prints of the man who had passed that way. It had been a small person, light of weight and light of step – short and measured paces. Surprisingly, the shoes were in fair repair. He was evidently well-fed and clear of mind because his steps marched the ground without faltering. The right foot was sunk a trifle deeper than the left, indicating perhaps that the traveller was carrying something on that side. He had made no effort to cover his tracks.

Gary pursed his lips. Another trap.

Only the dumb, the unskilled or the over-eager would follow the inviting footprints of the well-fed traveller. Only a desperately starving man would rush headlong after the steps, seeking their wealthy owner. He would never live to find him of course. The trail would lead into a town, or the tracker would circle around and double back on his own tracks to wait for the unlucky man following them. Well-fed men stayed that way by living on the hopes of those whose misfortune it was to have trailed them.

These footprints led into the town.

Gary crept nearer and stretched out flat on his belly to

study the place. Nothing moved along its streets and there was no betraying curl of smoke from a chimney. An hour went by, and then another. He heard no sound of moving doors, no scraping of shoes on wood, no noise whatever. Towards noon the wind shifted, bringing the smell of the town to him and also bringing the promise of more snow. Carefully he raised his head to sniff the wind. There was no odour of fresh blood, of newly killed game. The firing of the rifle had been but a part of the trap.

The well-fed traveller, new to this region, had journeyed across the plain and left his visible marks behind him. He had fired the rifle to attract attention of any who might be in the vicinity and was now lying in ambush for anyone who stupidly followed. Gary searched the area around him but there was no one other than himself reaching for the bait.

He waited without movement for the snow that was coming.

In mid-afternoon it began to fall, lightly at first and then the flakes grew heavier and larger, falling with a steadiness that indicated it would continue for some time. It was not too cold. The clouded sky darkened and shortly before the unseen sunset a heavy fall began in earnest. The lump he made on the ground was soon blanketed over, merging into the white surrounding night. From a distance – the distance to the nearest building – his body was no more than a shapeless bulge in the snow.

Patiently, Gary waited for sight or sound or smell of the bait.

The scent brought him fully awake.

The snow had long since stopped and the utter darkness of late night engulfed the world, leaving only that faint illumination close to the ground. Gary had been dozing, almost sleeping with his eyes warily open and his face twisted to catch the vagrant drift of wind, when the scent came. It floated to him downwind from the town and he shut his eyes in an effort to force identification. There was no surface memory to name it, no quick cataloguing to identify the scent displayed by the bait. It remained elusive, tantalising.

He recognised it as none of the variety of clothes or skins

man now wore to cover his body, none of the combustibles used for fire, no possible kind of food he had ever smelled or sampled. It was not the peculiar odorous fumes given off by that lone truck traversing the highway, nor was it of any animal across the face of the silent land. The scent had come suddenly, as if emerging from a doorway, and after a few brief moments it had gone away again, as if behind a closed door. Oddly, there had been no mingling scents, no accompanying smell of leather or wool clothing, no smoke of tobacco, nothing but *it* alone.

Then, in the next half hour, came wood smoke.

Gary continued to watch and wait but the smoke was invisible in the night air. The peculiar scent did not come again.

He realised it would be foolish to wait until dawn for then he could only retreat from the town; if anything was to be gained, if he was to go in after the bait at all, he would have to do it now under the cover of darkness. And if the bait *knew* he was waiting, the queer scent and the wood smoke were designed to draw him in quickly. If it did not know, it was sheer carelessness. Gary listened only a moment longer to his demanding stomach, and moved forward.

Rising up from the ground he crept nearer the town, taking care not to dislodge the snow clinging to his back. The smell of smoke grew stronger as he approached the buildings and presently he located the source, the tumbling chimney of an old brick house situated on the very edge of the field he was crossing. Briefly thankful that he did not have to enter the town proper, he came up close to the house, circled it, watched it, listened to it.

At the door he found prints in the snow, prints placed there since the fall had ceased. They were small, narrow prints of bare feet – much smaller than the shoes which had left the trail the day before. Gary backed away from them, crept around to the far side of the house again and paused at the chimney. The bricks were warm, absorbing the heat of the crackling fire within. Presently he detected another sound, a fainter one that after long minutes of study revealed itself as boiling water. A fire in the fireplace and a pot of boiling water – and who would prepare a meal in the dead of night? Who would betray themselves with wood smoke, who would stand barefoot in the snow and let that strange scent mingle with the wind?

Moving cautiously along to a boarded-up window, Gary put his nostrils to the cracks.

Fire, warmth, excretion, no discernible odour from the bubbling pot – and very strongly, that puzzling scent.

A woman wearing perfume.

Abruptly there was a movement within the room and he fell to the ground, poorly covered because the snow no longer clung to him. He readied the rifle and waited.

Very slowly, very cautiously the door opened again and he knew those naked feet were standing in the doorway once more, perhaps stepping out into the snow itself so that she might better search the field where he had lain – and so that he might gain a better view and scent of her. The bait was quite aware that he had followed, and had prepared herself accordingly.

He inched along silently towards the corner of the house, working a heavy-handle knife out of his belt and stopping just out of sight at the corner until she should close the door again, until those naked feet should return to the fireplace for warmth. Until her back was turned and she was off guard. Gary flung a swift glance around to search for possible movement – he was convinced the town was empty, else something would have happened when she first exposed herself. He and a strange woman, alone in the town, alone in the loud silence – how long had it been since that last occurred?

He snapped to attention. There was a soft whisper of sound as the door closed, the faint slap of her bare feet moving across the floor.

He jumped from his crouch at the corner of the house and sped for the door, holding the knife by its long wicked blade. He knew where she would be, knew she would be coming to a stop before the fireplace, her back to him. With a leap and a swing of his foot he kicked the door open, threw the reversed knife at the same instant and dropped prone across the sill, to prevent the door from closing on the rebound. The hilt thudded against the back of her skull.

The woman fell without sound escaping her lips, her rifle clattering to the floor beside the limp body.

Again Gary swung around to search the street and the town behind him, but nothing stirred. He scrambled inside, shut and barred the door. Crossing over to the woman, he seized the rifle and emptied it of its ammunition, tossing the now useless weapon at her feet. Finally, stepping over her prone body, he spilled the kettle of boiling water on to the fire, dousing the tell-tale heat and smoke.

Only then did he step back to look at her.

Her clothing had been neatly piled beside the fireplace, her shoes and a heavy black bag rested on the floor beside them. Gary moved swiftly over to the bag, seized his knife from the floor and slit a long gash in its side. The raw, partly frozen remains of a rabbit tumbled through the slit and he promptly scooped it up, to sink his teeth into the cold flesh. Following the exit of the rabbit, a thin trickle of sparkling glass beads dribbled out of the bag. Astonished, Gary dug his fingers into the interior and pulled out a fistful of the things, shiny pebbles that gleamed dully in the darkened room.

He moved across to the woman's body, turned her over on her back to stare down into her quiet face.

She was *much* older than nineteen now.

After a while he went to the door and got snow to rub in her face, to bring her back to consciousness. While he waited for her to revive, gently massaging her head and the back of her neck, he speculated on their future together. She could be of high value in the struggle to stay alive, could be the most tempting bait possible to trap men – as she had only recently demonstrated. She could be of very great use to him. And if she did her job well, perhaps he would forgive her the kettle of boiling water she had prepared. And there was *that* angle – it wouldn't be safe for him to let her grow hungry again.

He glanced down into her face, seeing her lids aflutter with the slow return of consciousness. Gary reflected that he'd have to find a new place to live – she'd certainly object to the cave. He grinned at the girl but it was lost in his heavy beard.

Her eyes were the same wide, brilliant blue they had been the first time he'd seen them, her face the same frightened image he had first known. Only her body had changed in the ten years.

'Hello, nineteen . . . remember me?'

WILSON TUCKER

THE LINCOLN HUNTERS

Not everyone fitted comfortably into the prim and puritanical world of the 26th century; but sadly, for the vast majority, the dream of travelling back to more congenial times remained just that: a dream.

Not so, however, for Benjamin Steward. As head of a team of Time Researchers, Steward had a welcome escape route from the authoritarian rigours of the year 2578. So when he was offered the job of obtaining a recording of a famous 'lost' speech made by Abraham Lincoln in 1856, he naturally jumped at the chance.

But very soon Steward sensed that somewhere along the line the mission had gone disastrously wrong – and it would take all his courage and ingenuity to prevent the dream of time-travel from turning into a nightmare that might never end . . .

CORONET BOOKS

JOHN WYNDHAM

THE SECRET PEOPLE

The planners of the world's greatest engineering feat – the flooding of part of the Sahara desert – knew nothing of the life which now struggled for survival below their New Sea. But an unexpected accident in his stratoplane plunged Mark Sunnet and his girlfriend Margaret into a terrifyingly different world. A vast maze of caverns lay hundreds of feet below the water, inhabited by the descendants of an ancient human race.

A crude carving on the rock walls was Margaret's salvation. With Bast, the desert cat, she was treated like a goddess resurrected from the past. But the waters were rising. It would not be long before she and Mark faced death with their doomed captors . . .

CORONET BOOKS

ROBERT SILVERBERG

SHADRACH IN THE FURNACE

The year is 2012. The world lies ravaged by biological warfare, its population decimated by a ferocious genetically-transmitted disease known as the organ rot. And presiding over the ruins is a ninety-three-year-old tyrant, preserved in a state of youth by a series of organ transplants: the self-styled Genghis Mao.

Shadrach Mordecai, Genghis Mao's trusted personal physician, was a vital cog in the great machine devoted to keeping the ruler alive: linked to him by a network of electronic implants, Shadrach was able to detect and diagnose the first signs of malfunction in his lord and master. But close as he was to the ageing dictator, Shadrach could not have known that events would soon plunge him into a desperate struggle – a struggle in which a paragon of idealism faced the very incarnation of evil.

CORONET BOOKS